Hamilton Wright Mabie

Under the Trees and Elsewhere

Hamilton Wright Mabie

Under the Trees and Elsewhere

ISBN/EAN: 9783743303379

Manufactured in Europe, USA, Canada, Australia, Japa

Cover: Foto ©Andreas Hilbeck / pixelio.de

Manufactured and distributed by brebook publishing software
(www.brebook.com)

Hamilton Wright Mabie

Under the Trees and Elsewhere

UNDER THE TREES AND ELSEWHERE * BY HAMILTON WRIGHT MABIE

NEW YORK : PUBLISHED BY
DODD, MEAD AND COMPANY
.MDCCCXCVI

TO

MY FRIENDS IN ARDEN,

C. B. Y.

AND

M. Y. W.

CONTENTS.

viii CONTENTS.

UNDER THE TREES

AND ELSEWHERE.

CHAPTER I.

AN APRIL DAY.

My study has been a dull place of late ; even
the open fire, which still lingers on the hearth, has
failed to exorcise a certain gray and weary spirit
which has somehow taken possession of the prem-
ises. As I was thinking this morning about the
best way of ejecting this unwelcome inmate, it suddenly occurred to me that for some time past my
study has been simply a workshop ; the fire has
been lighted early and burned late, the windows
have been closed to keep out all disturbing sounds,
and the pile of manuscript on the table has steadily
grown higher and higher. "After all," I said to
myself, " it is I that ought to be ejected." Acting
on this conclusion, and without waiting for the service of process of formal dislodgment, I have let
the fire go out, opened the windows, locked the
door, and put myself into the hands of my old
friend, Nature, for refreshment and society. I find

in vain when skies are softer and the green roof
has been stretched over the woodland ways. In
fact, one can hardly lay claim to any intimacy with
Nature until he loves her best when she discards
her royalty, and, like Cinderella, clad only in the
cast-off garments of sunnier days, she crouches before the ashes of the faded year. The test of
friendship is its fidelity when every charm of fortune and environment has been swept away, and
the bare, undraped character alone remains ; if love
still holds steadfast, and the joy of companionship
survives in such an hour, the fellowship becomes a
beautiful prophecy of immortality. To all profes-
sions of love Nature applies this infallible test with
a kind of divine impartiality. With the first note
of the bluebird, under the brief flush of an April
sky, her alluring invitation goes forth to the world ;
day by day she deepens the blue of her summer
skies and fills them with those buoyant clouds that
float like dreams across the vision of the waking
day ; night after night she touches the stars with a
softer radiance, and breathes upon her roses so that
they are eager for the dawn, that they may lay
their hearts open to her gaze ; the forests take on
more and more the lavish mood of the summer,
until they have buried their great trunks in perpetual shade. The splendid pageant moves on,
gathering its votaries as it passes from one marvelous change to another ; and yet the Mistress of the
Revels is nowhere visible. The crowds press from

point to point, peering into the depths of the woods and watching stealthily where the torrent breaks from its dungeon in the hills, and leaps, mad with joy, in the new-found liberty of light and motion ; but not a flutter of her garment betrays to the keenest eye the Presence which is the soul of all this visible, moving scene.

And now there is a subtle change in the air ; premonitions of death begin to thrust themselves in the midst of the revelry ; there is a brief hush, a sudden glow of splendor, and, lo ! the pageant is seemingly at an end. The crowd linger a little, gather a few faded leaves, and depart ; a few— a very few—wait. Now that the throngs have vanished and the revelry is over, they are conscious of a deep, pervading quietude ; these are days when something touches them with a sense of near and sacred fellowship ; Nature has cast aside her gifts, and given herself. For there is a something behind the glory of summer, and they only have entered into real communion with Nature who have learned to separate her from all her miracles of power and beauty ; who have come to understand that she lives apart from the singing of birds, the blossoming of flowers, and the waving of branches heavy with leaves.

. The Greeks saw some things clearly without seeing them deeply ; they interpreted through a beautiful mythology all the external phenomena of Nature. The people of the farther East, on the other hand, saw more obscurely, but far more deeply; they looked less at the visible things which Nature held out to them, and more into the mysteries of her hidden processes, her silent but universal mutations; the subtle vanishings and re-appearings of her presence; they seemed to hear the mighty loom on which the seasons are woven, to feel through some primitive but forgotten kin-ship the throes of the birth-hour, the vigils of suffering, and the agonies of death. Was there not in such an attitude toward Nature a hint of the only real fellowship with her?

CHAPTER II.

UNDER THE APPLE BOUGHS.

FOR weeks past I have been conscious of some mystery in the air ; there have been fleeting signs of secret communication between earth and sky, as if the hidden powers were in friendly league and some great concerted movement were on foot. There have been soft lights playing upon the tender grass on the lawn, and caressing those delicate hues through which each individual tree and shrub searches for its summer foliage ; the mornings have slipped so quietly in through the eastern gates, and the afternoons have vanished so softly across the western hills, that one could not but suspect a plot to avert attention and lull watchful eyes into negligence while all things were made ready for the moment of revelation. At times a subdued light has filled the broad arch of heaven, and, later, a fringe of rain has moved gently across the low hills and fallow fields, rippling like a wave from that upper sea which hangs invisible in golden weather, but becomes portentous and vast as the nether seas when the clouds gather and the celestial watercourses are unlocked. One day I thought I saw signs of a falling out between the conspirators, and I set myself to watch for some disclosure which might escape from one side or the other in the frankness of anger. The earth was sullen and overcast, the sky dark and forbidding, the clouds rolled together and grew black, and the shadows deepened upon the grass. At last there was a vivid flash of lightning, a crash of thunder, and the sudden roar of rain. " Now," I said to myself, " I shall learn what all this secrecy has been about." But I was doomed to disappointment ; after a few minutes of angry expostulation the sky suddenly uncovered itself, the clouds piled themselves against the horizon and disclosed their silver linings, and over the whole earth there spread a broad smile, as if the hypocritical performance had been part of the original deception. I am confident now that it was, for that brief drenching of trees and sward was almost the last noticeable preparation before the curtain rose. The next day there · was a deep, unbroken quiet across our piece of world, as if a fragment of eternity had been quietly slipped into the place of one of our brief, noisy days. The trees stood motionless, as if awaiting some signal, and I listened in vain for that inarticulate and half-heard murmur of coming life which, day and night, had filled my thoughts these past weeks, and set the march of the hours to a sublime rhythm.

The next morning a faint perfume stole into my room. I rose hastily, ran to the window, and lo !

the secret was out: the apple trees were in bloom! Three days later, and the miracle so long in preparation was accomplished ; the slowly rising tide of life had broken into a foam of blossoms and buried the world in a billowy sea. There will come days of greater splendor than this, days of deeper foliage, of waving grain and ripening fruit, but no later day will eclipse this vision of paradise which lies outspread from my window ; life touches to-day the zenith of its earliest and freshest bloom ; tomorrow the blossoms will begin to sift down from the snowy branches, and the great movement of summer will advance again ; but for one brief day the year pauses and waits, reluctant to break the spell of this perfect hour, to mar by the stir of a single leaf the stainless loveliness of this revelation of nature's unwasted youth.

I do not care to look through these great masses of bloom ; it is enough simply to live in an hour which brings such an overflow of beauty from the ancient fountains ; but nature herself lures one to deeper thoughts, and, through the vision which spreads like a mirage over the landscape, hints at some hidden loveliness at the root of this riotous blossoming, some diviner vision for the eye of the spirit alone. "Look," she seems to say, as I stand and gaze with unappeased hunger of soul, "this is my holiday. In the coming weeks I have a whole race to feed, and over the length of the world men are imploring my help. They do their little share of work, and while they wait, waking and sleeping, anxiously watching winds and clouds, I vitalize their toil and turn all my forces to their bidding. The labor of the year is at hand and on its threshold I take this holiday. To-day I give you a glimpse of paradise; a garden in which all manner of loveliness blooms simply from the overflow of life, without thought, or care, or toil. This was my life before men came with their cries of hunger and nakedness; this shall be my life again when they have passed beyond. This which lies before you like a dream is a glimpse of life as it is in me, and shall be in you; immortal, inexhaustible fullness of power and beauty, overflowing in frolic loveliness. This shall be to you a day out of eternity, a moment out of the immortal youth to which all true life comes at last, and in which it abides."

I cannot say that I heard these words, and yet they were as real to me as if they had been audible; in all fellowship with Nature silence is deeper and more real than speech. As I stood meditating on these deep things that lie at the bottom of this sea of bloom, I understood why men in all ages have connected the flowering of the apple with their dreams of paradise; I saw at a glance the immortal symbolism of these blossoming fields and hillsides. I did not need to lift my eyes to look upon that garden of Hesperides, lying like a dream of heaven under the golden western skies, whence

Heracles brought back the fruit of Juno ; I asked no aid of Milton's imagination to see the mighty hero in

> . . . the gardens fair
> Of Hesperus and his daughters three,
> That sing about the golden tree ;

and as I gazed, the vision of that other and nobler hero came before me, whose purity is more to us than his prowess, and who waits in Avilion, the " Isle of Apples," for the call that shall summon him back from Paradise.

> I am going a long way
> With these thou seest—if indeed I go
> (For all my mind is clouded with a doubt)—
> To the island-valley of Avilion ;
> Where falls not hail, or rain, or any snow,
> Nor even wind blows loudly ; but it lies
> Deep-meadow'd, happy, fair with orchard lawns
> And bowery hollows crown'd with summer sea,
> Where I will heal me of my grievous wound.

CHAPTER III.

ALONG THE ROAD.

I.

SINCE I turned the key on my study I have almost forgotten the familiar titles on which my eye rested whenever I took a survey of my book-shelves. Those friends stanch and true, with whom I have held such royal fellowship when skies were chill and winds were cold, will not forget me, nor shall I become unfaithful to them. I have gone abroad that I may return later with renewed zest and deeper insight to my old companionships. Books and nature are never inimical ; they mutually speak for and interpret each other ; and only he who stands where their double light falls sees things in true perspective and in right relations.

The road along whose winding course I have been making a delightful pilgrimage to-day has the double charm of natural beauty and of human association ; it is old, as age is reckoned in this new world ; it has grown hard under the tread of sleeping generations, and the great figures of history have passed over it in their journeys between the two great cities which mark its limits. In the earlier days it was the king's high-way, and along its up-hill and down-dale course the battalions of royal troops marched and counter-marched to the call of bugles that have gone silent these hundred years and more. It is a road of varied fortunes, like many of those who have passed over it ; it is sometimes rich in all manner of price-less possessions, and again it is barren, poverty-stricken and desolate. It climbs long hills, some-times in a roundabout, hesitating, half-hearted way, and sometimes with an abrupt and breathless ascent ; at the summit it seems to pause a moment as if to invite the traveler to survey the splendid domain which it commands. On one side, in such a restful moment, one sees the wide circle of waters, stretching far off to a horizon which rests on clus-ters of islands and marks the limits of the world ; in the foreground, and sweeping around the other points of the compass, a landscape rich in foliage, full of gentle undulations, and dotted here and there with fallow fields, spreads itself like another sea that has been hushed into sudden immutability, and then sown, every wave and swell of it, with the seeds of exhaustless fertility.

From such points of eminence as these the road sometimes runs with hurried descent, as if longing for solitude, into the heart of the woodlands, and there winds slowly and solemnly under the over-shadowing branches ; there are no fences here, and the sharp lines of separation between road-bed and

forest were long ago erased in that quiet usurpa-
tion of man's work, which Nature never fails to
make the moment she is left to herself. The
ancient spell of the woods is unbroken in this leafy
solitude, and no traveler in whom imagination survives can hope to escape it. The deep breathings
of primeval life are almost audible, and one feels in
a quick and subtle perception the long past which
unites him with the earliest generations and the
most remote ages.

Passing out from this brief worship under the
arches of the most venerable roof in Christendom,
the road takes on a frolic mood and courts the
open meadows and the flooding sunshine ; green,
sweet, and strewn with wild flowers, the open fields
call one from either side, and arrest one's feet at
every turn with solicitations to freedom and joyous-
ness. The white clouds in the blue sky and the long
sweep of these radiant meadows conspire together
to persuade one that time has strayed back to its
happy childhood again, and that nothing remains of
the old activities but play in these immortal fields.
Here the carpet is spread over which one runs with
childish heedlessness, courting the disaster which
brings him back to the breast of the old mother,
and makes him feel once more the warmth and
sweetness out of which all strength and beauty
spring. A little brook crosses the road under a
rattling bridge, and wanders on across the fields,
limpid and rippling, running its little strain of music

through the silence of the meadows. Its voice is the only sound which breaks the stillness, and that itself seems part of the solitude. By day the clouds marshal their shadows on it, and when night comes the heavens sow it with stars, until it flows like a dissolving belt of sky through the fragrant darkness. Sometimes, as I have come this way after nightfall, I have heard its call across the invisible fields, and in the sound I have heard I know not what of deep and joyous mystery ; the long-past and the far-off future whispering together, under cover of the night, of those things which the stars remember from their youth, and to which they look forward in some remote cycle of their shining.

Past old and well-worked farms, into which the toil and thrift of generations have gone, the old road leads me, and brings my thoughts back from elemental forces and primeval ages to these later centuries in which human life has overlaid these hills and vales with rich memories. Wherever man goes Nature makes room for him, as if prepared for his coming, and ready to put her mighty shoulder to the wheel of his prosperity. The old fences, often decayed and fallen, are not spurned ; the movement of universal life does not flow past them and leave them to rot in their ugliness ; year by year time stains them into harmony with the rocks, and every summer a wave out of the great sea of life flings itself over them, and leaves behind some slight and seemly garniture of moss and vine. The

old farmhouses have grown into the landscape, and
the hurrying road widens its course, and sometimes
makes a long detour, that it may unite these outlying folk with the great world.   There stands the
old school-house, sacred to every traveler who has
learned that childhood is both a memory and a
prophecy of heaven.   One pauses here, and hears,
in the unbroken stillness, the rush of feet that have
never grown weary with travel, and the clamor of
voices through which immortal youth still shouts to
the kindred hills and skies.   Into those windows
nature throws all manner of invitations, and
through them she gets only glances of recognition
and longing.   There are the fields, the woods, and
the hills in one perpetual rivalry of charm ; the
bird sings in the bough over the window, and on
still afternoons the brook calls and calls again.
Here one feels anew the eternal friendship between
childhood and Nature, and remembers that they only
can abide in that fellowship who carry into riper
years the self-forgetfulness, the sweet unconsciousness, the open mind and heart of a child.

CHAPTER IV.

ALONG THE ROAD.

II.

I HAVE found that walking stimulates observation and opens one's eyes to movements and appearances in earth and sky, which ordinarily escape attention. The constant change of landscape which attends even the slow progress of a loitering gait puts one on the alert for discoveries of all kinds, and prompts one to suspect every leafy covert and to peer into every wooded recess with the expectation of surprising Nature as Actæon surprised Diana —in the moment of uncovered loveliness. On the other hand, when one lounges by the hour in the depths of the forest, or sits, book in hand, under the knotted and familiar apple tree, on a summer afternoon, the faculty of observation is lulled into a dreamless sleep ; one ceases to be far enough away from Nature to observe her ; one becomes part of the great, silent movements in the midst of which he sits, mute and motionless, while the hours slip by with the peace of eternity already upon them.

When I reached the end of my walk, and paused

for a moment before retracing my steps, I was conscious of the inexhaustible richness of the world
through which I had come ; a thousand voices had
spoken to me, and a thousand sights of wonder
moved before me ; I was awake to the universe
which most of us see only in broken and unintelli-
gent dreams.   Through all this realm of truth and
poetry men have passed and repassed these many
years, I said to myself ; and I began to wonder
how many of those now long asleep really saw or
heard this great glad world of sun and summer !
I began slowly to retrace my steps, and as I reached
the summit of the hill and looked beyond I saw
the cattle standing knee-deep in the brook that
loiters across the fields, and I heard the faint
bleating of sheep borne from a distant pasturage.

These familiar sights and sounds touched me
with a sudden pathos; there is nothing in human
associations so venerable, so familiar, as the lowing
of the home-coming kine and the bleating of the
flocks.   They carry one back to the first homes and
the most ancient families. Older than history,
more ancient than civilization, are these familiar
tones which unite the low-lying meadows and the
upland pastures with the fire on the hearth-stone
and the nightly care of the fold. When the
shadows deepen over the country-side, the oldest
memories are revived and the oldest habits recalled
by the scenes about the farm-house. The same
offices fall to the husbandman, the same sights re-

veal themselves to the housewife, the same sounds, mellow with the resonance of uncounted centuries, greet the ears of the children as in the most primitive ages.

The highway itself stands as a memorial of the most venerable customs and the most ancient races. As I lift my eyes from its beaten road-bed, and look out upon it through the imagination, it escapes all later boundaries and runs back through history to the very dawn of civilization; it marks the earliest contact of men with a world which was wrapped in mystery. The hour that saw a second home built by human hands heard the first footfall on the first highway. That narrow foot-path led to civilization, and has broadened into the highway because human fellowships and needs have multiplied and directed the countless feet that have beaten it into permanency. Every new highway has been a new bond between Nature and men, a new evidence of that indissoluble fellowship into which they are forever united.

I have sometimes tried to recall in imagination the world of Nature before a human voice had broken the silence or a human foot left its impress on the soil; but when I remember that what I see in this sweep of force and beauty is largely what I myself put into the vision, that Nature without the human ear is soundless, and without the human eye colorless, I understand that what lies spread before me never was until a human soul confronted it and became its interpreter. This radiant world upon which I look was without form and void until the earliest man brought to the vision of it that creative power within himself which touched it with form and color and relations not its own. Nature is as incomplete and helpless without man as man would be without Nature. He brought her varied and inexhaustible beauty, and clothed her with a garment woven on we know not what looms of divine energy ; and she fed, sheltered, and strengthened him for the life which lay before him. Together they have wrought from the first hour, and civilization, with all the circle of its arts, is their joint handiwork.

In the atmosphere of our rich modern fellowship with Nature, the unwritten poetry to which every open heart falls heir, we forget our earliest dependence on the great mother and the lessons she taught when men gathered about her knee in the childhood of the world. Not a spade turned the soil, not an ax felled a tree, not a path was made through the forest, that did not leave, in the man whose arm put forth the toil, some moral quality. In the obstacles which she placed in their pathway, in the difficulties with which she surrounded their life, the wise mother taught her children all the lessons which were to make them great. It was no easy familiarity which she offered them, no careless bestowal of bounty upon dependents ; she met them as men, and offered them a perpetual alliance upon

such terms as great and equal sovereigns proffer
and accept.   She gave much, but she asked even
more than she offered, and in the first moment of
intercourse she struck in men that lofty note of
sovereignty which has never ceased to thrill the race
with mysterious tones of power and prophecy.
Men have stood erect and fearless in the presence
of the most awful revelations of the forces of
Nature, affirming by their very attitude a supremacy
of spirit which no preponderance of power can
overshadow.   Face to face through all his history
man has stood with Nature, and to each generation
she has opened some new page of her inexhaustible
story.   Beginning in the hardest toil for the most
material rewards, this fellowship has steadily added
one province of knowledge and intimacy after
another, until it has become inclusive of the most
delicate and hidden recesses of character as well as
those which are obvious and primary.   In response
to spirits which have continually come into a closer
contact with her life, Nature has added to her gifts
of food and wine, poetry and art, far-reaching
sciences, occult wisdoms and skills; she has invited
the greatest to become her ministers, and has
rewarded their unselfish service by sharing with
them the mighty forces that sleep and awake at her
bidding; one after another the poets of truest gift
have forsaken the beaten paths of cities and men,
and found along her untrodden ways the vision that
never fades; her voice, now that men begin to

understand it again as their forefathers understood
it, is a voice of worship.   So, from their first work
for food and shelter, men have steadily won from
Nature gifts of insight and knowledge and prophecy,
until now the mightiest secrets are whispered by the
trees to him who listens, and the winds sometimes
take up the burden of prophecy and sing of a
fellowship in which all truth shall be a common
possession.

As I walk along the old highway, the deepening
shadows touch the familiar landscape with mystery ;
one landmark after another vanishes until the
lights in the scattered farm-houses gleam like reflected constellations.   A deep silence fills the
great heavens and broods over the wide earth; all
things have become dim and strange ; and yet I
feel no loneliness in the midst of this star-lit solitude.   The heavens shining over me, and the scattered household fires declare to me that fellowship
of light in which Nature holds out her hand to man
and leads him, step by step, to the unspeakable
splendors of her central sun.

CHAPTER V.

ONE of the sights upon which my eyes rest oftenest and with deepest content is a broad sweep of meadow slowly climbing the western sky until it pauses at the edge of a noble piece of woodland. It is a playground of wind and flowers and waving grasses. There are, indeed, days when it lies cold and sad under inhospitable skies, but for the most part the heavens are in league with cloud and sun to protect its charm against all comers. When the turf is fresh, all the promise of summer is in its tender green ; a little later, and it is sown thick with daisies and buttercups ; and as the breeze plays upon it these frolicsome flowers, which have known no human tending, seem to chase each other in endless races over the whole expanse. I have seen them run breathlessly up the long slope, and then suddenly turn and rush pell-mell down again. If the wind had only stopped for a moment its endless gossip with the leaves, I am sure I should have heard the gleeful shouts, the sportive cries, of these vagrant flowers whose spell is rewoven over every generation of children, and whose un-

23

studied beauty and joy recall, with every summer, some of the clews which most of us have lost in our journey through life.   Even as I write, I see the white and yellow heads tossing to and fro in a mood of free and buoyant being, which has for me, face to face with the problems of living, an unspeakable pathos.

What a depth of tender color fills the arch of heaven as it bends over this playground of the blooming and beauty-laden forces of nature !   The great summer clouds, shaping their courses to invisible harbors across the trackless aerial sea, love to drop anchor here and slowly trail their mighty shadows, vainly groping for something that shall make them fast.   The winds, that have come roaring through the woodlands, subdue their harsh voices and linger long in their journey across this sunny expanse.   It is true, they sing no lullabies as in the hollow under the hill where they themselves often fall asleep, but the music to which they move has a magical cadence of joy in it, and sets our thought to the dancing mood of the flowers.

Sometimes, on quiet afternoons, when the great world of work has somehow seemed to drop its burdens into space, and carries nothing but rest and quietude along its journey under the summer sky, I have seen a pageant in the open fields that has made me doubt whether a dream had not taken me unawares.   I have seen the first sweet flowers of spring rise softly out of the grass where they had been hiding, and call gently to each other, as if afraid that a single loud word would dissolve the charm of sun and warm breeze for which they had waited so long. After their dreamless sleep of months, these beautiful children of Mother Earth seemed almost afraid to break the stillness from which they had come, and strayed about noiselessly, with subdued and lovely mien, exhaling a perfume as delicate as themselves. Then, with a rush and shout, the summer flowers suddenly burst upon the scene, overflowing with life and merriment ; in lawless troops they ran hither and thither, flinging echoes of their laughter over the whole country-side, and soon overshadowing entirely their older and more sensitive fellows ; these, indeed, soon vanish altogether, as if lonely and out of place under the broad glare and high colors of midsummer. And now for weeks together the game went on without pause or break ; the revelry grew fast and furious, until one suspected that some night the Bacchic throng had passed that way and left their mood of wild and lawless frolic behind.

At last a softer aspect spread itself over the glowing sky and earth. The nights grew vocal with the invisible chorus of insect life ; there was a mellow splendor in the moonlight, which touched the distant hills and wide-spreading waters with a pathetic prophecy of change. And now, ripe, serene, and rich with the accumulated beauty of the summer, the autumn flowers appeared. Their movement was like the stately dances of olden times ; youth and its overflow were gone forever ; but in the hour of maturity there remained a noble beauty, which touched all imaginations and communicated to all visible things a splendor of which the most radiant hours of early summer had been only faintly prophetic. In the calm of these golden days the autumn flowers reigned with a more than regal state, and when the first cold breath of winter touched them, they fell from their great estate silently and royally as if their fate were matched to their rank. And now the fields were bare once more.

From such a dream as this I often awake joyfully to find the drama still in its first act, and to feel still before me the ever-deepening interest and ever-widening beauty of the miracle play to which Nature annually bids us welcome. Across this noble playground, with its sweep of landscape and its arch of sky, I often wander with no companions but the flowers, and with no desire for other fellowship. Here, as in more secluded and quiet places, Nature confides to those who love her some deep and precious truths never to be put into words, but ever after to rise at times over the horizon of thought like vagrant ships that come and go against the distant sea line, or like clouds that pass along the remotest circle of the sky as it sleeps upon the hills. The essence of play is the unconscious overflow of life that seeks escape in perfect self-forgetfulness. There is no effort in it, no whip of the will driving the unwilling energies to an activity from which they shrink ; one plays as the bird sings and the brook runs and the sun shines—not with conscious purpose, but from the simple over-flow. In this sense Nature never works, she is always at play. In perfect unconsciousness, with-out friction or effort, her mightiest movements are made and her sublimest tasks accomplished. Throughout the whole range of her activity one never comes upon any trace of effort, any sign of weariness ; one is always impressed—as Ruskin said long ago of works of genius—that he is stand-ing in the presence, not of a great effort, but of a great power ; that what has been done is only a single manifestation of the play of an inexhaustible force. There is somewhere in the universe an in-finite fountain of life and beauty which overflows and floods all worlds with divine energy and loveli-ness. When the tide recedes it pauses but a mo-ment, and then the music of its returning waves is heard along all shores, and its shining edges move irresistibly on until they have bathed the roots of the solitary flower on the highest Alp.

It is this divine method of growth which Nature opposes to our mechanisms ; it is this inexhaustible life, overflowing in unconsciousness and boundless fulness, that she forever reveals. The truth which underlies these two great facts needs no application to human life. Blessed, indeed, are they who live in it, and have caught from it something of the joy, the health, and the perennial beauty of Nature.

CHAPTER VI.

EARTH AND SKY.

IN nature, as in art, it is the sky which makes the landscape. Given the identical fields, woods, and retreating hills, and every change of sky, every modulation of light, will produce a new landscape; in light and atmosphere are concealed those mysteries of color, of distance, and of tone which clothe the changeless features of the visible world with infinite variety and charm. This fruitful marriage of the upper and the lower firmaments is perhaps the oldest fact known to men; it was the earliest discovery of the first observer, it still is the most illusive and beautiful mystery in nature. The most ancient mythologies began with it, the latest books of science and natural observation are still dealing with it. Myths that are older than history portray it in lofty symbolism or in splendid histories that embody the primitive ideals of divinity and humanity; the latest poets and painters would fain touch their verse or their canvas with some luminous gleam from the heart of this perpetual miracle. The unbroken procession of the seasons changes month by month the relations of earth and sky; day and night all the water-courses of the world rise in

invisible moisture to a fellowship with the birds that
have passed on swift wing above their currents ;
the great outlying seas, that sound the notes of
their vast and passionate unrest upon the shores of
every continent, are continually drawn upward to
swell the invisible upper ocean which, out of its
mighty life, feeds every green and fruitful thing
upon the bosom of the earth. This movement of
the oceans upon the continents through the illimitable channels of the sky is, in some ways, the most
mysterious and the most sublime of those miracles
which each day testify to the presence and majesty
of that Spirit behind Nature of whom the greatest
of modern poets thought when he wrote :

> Thus at the roaring loom of time I ply
> And weave for God the robe thou seest Him by.

The vast inland grain fields, that stretch in unbroken procession from horizon to horizon, have
the seas at their roots not less truly than the fertile
soil out of which they spring ; the verdure upon
the mountain ranges, that keep unbroken solitude
at the heart of the continents, speaks forever of the
distant oceans which nourish it, and spread it like
a vesture over the barren heights. No traveler,
deep in the recesses of the remotest inland, ever
passes beyond the voice of that encircling ocean
which never died out of the ears of the ancient
Ulysses in the first Odyssey of wandering.

Two months ago the apple trees were white with

the foam of the upper sea ; to-day the roses have
brought into my little patch of garden the hues with
which sun and sea proclaimed their everlasting
marriage in the twilight of yester even. In the
deep, passionate heart of these splendid flowers,
fragrant since they bloomed in Sappho's hand centuries ago, this sublime wedlock is annually cele-
brated ; earth and sky meet and commingle in this
miracle of color and sweetness, and when I carry
this lovely flower into my study all the poets fall
silent ; here is a depth of life, a radiant outcome
from the heart of mysteries, a hint of unimagined
beauty, such as they have never brought to me in
all their seeking. They have had their visions and
made them music ; they have caught faint echoes
of rushing seas and falling tides ; the shadows of
mountains have fallen upon them with low whisperings of unspeakable things hidden in the unexplored
recesses of their solitudes ; they have searched the
limitless arch of heaven when it was sown with
stars, and glittered like " an archangel full pano-
plied against a battle day "; but in all their quest
the sublime unity of Nature, the fellowship of force
with force, of sea with sky, of moisture with light,
of form with color, has found at their hands no such
transcendent demonstration as this fragile rose,
which to-night brings from the great temple to this
little shrine the perfume and the royalty of obedi-
ence to the highest laws, and reverence for the
divinest mysteries. Here sky and earth and sea

meet in a union which no science can dissolve, because God has joined them together.   Could I but
penetrate the mystery which lies at the heart of this
fragile flower, I should possess the secret of the
universe ; I should understand the ancient miracle
which has baffled wisdom from the beginning and
will not discover itself to the end of time.

If I permit my thought to rest upon this fragrant
flower, to touch petal and stem and root, and unite
them with the vast world in which, by a universal
contribution of force, they have come to maturity,
I find myself face to face with the oldest and the
deepest questions men have ever sought to answer.
Elements of earth and sea and sky are blended here
in one of those forms of radiant and vanishing
beauty with which the unseen life of Nature crowns
the years in endless and inexhaustible profusion.
As it budded and opened into full flower in the
garden, how complete it seemed in itself, and how
isolated from all other visible things !   But in
reality how dependent it was, how entirely the creation of forces as far apart as earth and sky !   The
great tide from the Unseen cast it for a moment into
my possession ; for an hour it has filled a human
home with its far-brought sweetness ; to-morrow it
will fall apart and return whence it came.   As I look
into its heart of passionate color, the whole visible
universe, that seems so fixed and stable, becomes immaterial, evanescent, vanishing ; it is no longer a
permanent order of seas and continents and

rounded skies ; it is a vision painted by an unseen hand against a background of mystery. Dead, cold, unchangeable as I see it in the glimpses of a single hour, it becomes warm, vital, forever changing as I gaze upon it from the outlook of the centuries. It is the momentary creation of forces that stream through it in endless ebb and flow, that are to-day touching the sky with elusive splendor, and to-morrow springing in changeful loveliness from the depths of earth. The continents are transformed into the seas that encircle them ; the seas rise into the skies that overarch them ; the skies mingle with the earth, and send back from the uplifted faces of flowers greetings to the stars they have deserted. Mountains rise and sink in the sublime rhythm to which the movement of the universe is set ; that song without words still audible in the sacred hour when the morning stars announce the day, and the birds match their tiny melodies with the universal harmony.

In the unbroken vision of the centuries all things are plastic and in motion ; a divine energy surges through all; substantial for a moment here as a rock, fragile and vanishing there as a flower ; but everywhere the same, and always sweeping onward through its illimitable channel to its appointed end. It is this vital tide on which the universe gleams and floats like a mirage of immutability ; never the same for a single moment to the soul that contemplates it : a new creation each hour and to every

eye that rests upon it. No dead mechanism moves
the stars, or lifts the tides, or calls the flowers from
their sleep; truly this is the garment of Deity,
and here is the awful splendor of the Perpetual
Presence. It is the old story of the Greek Proteus
translated into universal speech. It is the song of
the Persian poet :

The sullen mountain, and the bee that hums,
   A flying joy, about its flowery base,
Each from the same immediate fountain comes,
   And both compose one evanescent race.

There is no difference in the texture fine
   That's woven through organic rock and grass,
And that which thrills man's heart in every line,
   As o'er its web God's weaving fingers pass.

The timid flower that decks the fragrant field,
   The daring star that tints the solemn dome,
From one propulsive force to being reeled;
   Both keep one law and have a single home.

CHAPTER VII.

THE MYSTERY OF NIGHT.

EVERY day two worlds lie at my door and invite me into mysteries as far apart as darkness and light. These two realms have nothing in common save a certain identity of form ; color, relation, distance, are lost or utterly changed. In the vast fields of heaven a still more complete and sublime transformation is wrought. It is a new hemisphere which hangs above me, with countless fires lighting the awful highways of the universe, and guiding the daring and reverent thought as it falters in the highest empyrean. The mind that has come into fellowship with Nature is subtly moved and penetrated by the decline of light and the oncoming of darkness. As the sun is replaced by the stars, so is the hot, restless, eager spirit of the day replaced by the infinite calm and peace of the night. The change does not come abruptly or with the suddenness of violent movement ; no dial is delicate enough to register the moment when day gives place to night. With that amplitude of power which accompanies every movement, with that sublime quietude of energy which pervades every action, Nature calls the day across the hills and summons the night that has been waiting at the eastern gates. No stir, no strife, no noise of great activities, put forth on a vast scale, break the spell of an hour which is the daily witness of a miracle, and waits, hushed and silent, in a world-wide worship, while the altar fires blaze on the western hills.

In that unspeakable splendor, earth and air and sea are for the moment one, and through them all there flashes a divine radiance ; time is not left without the witness of its sanctity as it fades off the dials of earth and slips like a shining rivulet into the shoreless sea of light beyond. The day that was born with seas and suns at its cradle is fol-lowed to its grave by the long procession of the stars. And now that it has gone, with its numberless activities, and the heat and stress of their conten-tions, how gently and irresistibly Nature summons her children back to herself, and touches the brow, hot with the fever of work, with the hand of peace ! An infinite silence broods over the fields and upon the restless bosom of the sea. Insensibly there steals into thought, spent and weary with many problems, a deep and sweet repose ; the soul does not sleep ; it returns to the ancient mother, and at her breast feels the old hopes revived, the old aspirations quickened, the old faiths relight their dying fires. The fever of agonizing struggle yields to the calm of infinite trust; the clouds fall apart and reveal the vision, that seemed lost, inviolate forever; the brief, fierce, fruitless strife for self is succeeded by an unquestioning trust in that universal good, above and beyond all thought, for which the universe stands. Who shall despair while the fields of earth are sown with flowers and the fields of heaven blossom with stars? The open heart knows, in a revelation which comes to it with every dawn and sunset, that life does not mock its children when it holds this cup of peace to their anguished lips, and that into this tideless sea of rest and beauty every breathless and turbulent streamlet flows at last.

In the silence of night how real and divine the universe becomes! Doubt and unbelief retreat before the awful voices that were silenced by the din of the day, but now that the little world of man is hushed, seem to have blended all sounds into themselves. Beyond the circle of trees, through which a broken vision of stars comes and goes with the evening wind, the broad earth lies hushed and hidden. Along the familiar road a new and mysterious charm is spread like a net that entangles the feet of every traveler and keeps him loitering on where he would have passed in unobservant haste by day. The great elms murmur in low, inarticulate tones, and the shadows at their feet hide themselves from the moon, moving noiselessly through all the summer night. The woods in the distance stand motionless in the wealth of their massed foliage, keeping guard over the unbroken

silence that reigns in all their branching aisles.
Beyond the far-spreading waters lie white and
dreamlike, and tempt the thought to the fairylands
that sleep just beyond the line of the horizon. A
sweet and restful mystery, like a bridal veil, hides
the face of Nature, and he only can venture to lift it
who has won the privilege by long and faithful devotion.

If the night be starlit the shadows are denser, the
outlook narrower, the mystery deeper ; but what a
vision overhangs the world and makes the night
sublime with the poetry of God's thought visible to
all eyes ! Who does not feel the passage of divine
dreams over his troubled life when the infinite
meadows of heaven are suddenly abloom with light ?
On such a night immortality is written on earth and
sky; in the silence and darkness there is no hint of
death ; a sweet and fragrant life seems to breathe
its subtle, inaudible music through all things. In
the depths of the woods one feels no loneliness; no
liquid note of hermit thrush is needed to make
that silence music. The harmony of universal
movement, rounded by one thought, carried forward by one power, guided to one end, is there for
those who will listen ; the mighty activities which
feed the century-girded oak from the invisible
chambers of air and the secret places of the earth
are so divinely adjusted to their work that one
shall never detect their toil by any sound of
struggle or by any sight of effort. Noiselessly, in-

visibly, the great world breathes new life into every
part of its being, while the darkness curtains it
from the fierce ardor of the day.

In the night the fountains are open and flowing ;
a marvelous freshness touches leaf and flower and
grass, and rebuilds their shattered loveliness. The
stars look down from their inaccessible heights on
a new creation, and as the procession of the hours
passes noiselessly on, it leaves behind a dewy fragrance which shall exhale before the rising sun,
like a universal incense, making the portals of the
morning sweet with prophecies of the flowers which
are yet to bloom, and the birds whose song still
sleeps with the hours it shall set to music. The
unbroken repose of Nature, born not of idleness
but of the perfect adjustment of immeasurable
forces to their task, becomes more real and com-
prehensible when the darkness hides the infinitude
of details, and leaves only the great massive
effects for the eye to rest upon. While men
sleep, the world sweeps silently onward under
the watchful stars, in a flight which makes no
sound and leaves no trace. Through the deep
shadows the mountains loom in solitary and
awful grandeur ; the wide seas send forth and
recall their mighty tides ; the continents lie
veiled in rolling mists ; the immeasurable universe glitters and burns to the farthest out-
skirts of space ; and yet, nestled amid this sublime activity, the little flower dreams of the day,

and in its sleep is ministered to as perfectly as if it were the only created thing.

When one stands on the shores of night and looks off on that mighty sea of darkness in which a world lies engulfed, there is no thought but worship and no speech but silence. Face to face with immensity and infinity, one travels in thought among the shining islands that rise up out of the fathomless shadows, and feels everywhere the stir of a life which knows no weariness and makes no sound, which pervades the darkness no less than the light, and makes the night glorious as the day with its garniture of constellations ; and even as one waits, speechless and awestruck, the morning star touches the edges of the hills, and a new day breaks resplendent in the eastern sky.

CHAPTER VIII

OFF SHORE.

WHO has not heard, amid the heat and din of cities, the voice of the sea striking suddenly into the hush of thought its penetrating note of mystery and longing? Then work and the fever which goes with it vanished on the instant, and in the crowded street or in the narrow room there rose the vision of unbroken stretches of sky, free winds, and the surge of the unresting waves. That invitation never loses its alluring power; no distance wastes its music, and no preoccupation silences its solicitation. It stirs the oldest memories, and awakens the most primitive instincts; the long past speaks through it, and through it the buried generations snatch a momentary immortality. History that has left no record, rich and varied human experiences that have no chronicle, rise out of the forgetfulness in which they are engulfed, and are puissant once more in the intense and irresistible longing with which the heart answers the call of the sea. Once more the blood flows with fuller pulse, the eye flashes with conscious freedom and power, the heart beats to the music of wind and wave, as in the days when the fathers of a long past spread sail

and sought home, spoil, or change upon the trackless waste. Into every past the sea has sometime
sounded its mighty note of joy or anguish, and
deep in every memory there remains some vision of
tossing waves that once broke on eyes long sealed.

All day the free winds have filled the heavens,
and flung here and there a handful of foam upon
the surface of the deep. No cloud has dimmed the
splendor of a day which has filled the round heavens
with soft music and touched the sea with strange and
changeful beauty. It has been enough to wait and
watch, to forget self, to escape the limitations of
personality, and to become part of the movement,
which, hour by hour, has passed through one marvelous change after another, until now it seems to
pause under the sleepless vigilance of the stars.
They look down from their immeasurable altitudes
on the vast expanse of which only a miniature hemisphere stretches before me. How wide and fathomless seems the ocean, even from a single isolated
point ! What infinite distances are only half veiled
by the distant horizon line ! What islands and
continents and undiscovered worlds lie beyond that
faint and ever receding circle where the sight
pauses, while the thought travels unimpeded on its
pathless way? There lies the untamed world which
brooks no human control, and preserves the primeval solitude of the epochs before men came ; there
are the elemental forces mingling and commingling in eternal fellowships and rivalries. There the

winds sweep, and the storms marshal their shadows as on the first day; there, too, the sunlight sleeps on the summer sea as it slept in those forgotten summers before a sail had ever whitened the blue, or a keel cut evanescent furrows in the trackless waste.

Every hour has brought its change to make this day memorable ; hour by hour the lights have transformed the waters and hung over them a sky full of varied and changeful radiance. Across the line of the distant horizon white sails have come and gone in broken and mysterious procession, and the imagination has followed them far in their unknown journeyings. As silently as they passed from sight, all human history enacted in this vast province of nature's empire has vanished, and left no trace of itself save here and there a bit of drift-wood. There lies the unconquered and forever inviolate kingdom of forces over which no human skill will ever cast the net of conquest.

The sea speaks to the imagination as no other aspect of the natural world does, because of its vastness, its immeasurable and overwhelming power, its exclusion from human history, its free, buoyant, changeful being. It stands for those strange and unfamiliar revelations with which nature sometimes breaks in upon our easy relation with her, and brings back on the instant that sense of remoteness which one feels when in intimate fellowship a friend suddenly lifts the curtain from

some great experience hitherto unsuspected. In
the vast sweep of life through Nature there must
always be aspects of awful strangeness ; great
realms of mystery will remain unexplored, and almost inaccessible to human thought ; days will
dawn at intervals in which those who love most and
are nearest Nature will feel an impenetrable cloud
over all things, and be suddenly smitten with a
sense of weakness ; the greatest of all her interpre-
ters are but children in knowledge of her mighty
activities and forces. On the sea this sense of remoteness and strangeness comes oftener than in
the presence of any other natural form ; even the
mountains make sheltered places for our thought at
their feet, or along their precipitous ledges ; but
the sea makes no concessions to our human weakness, and leaves the message which it intones with
the voice of tempest and the roar of surge without
an interpreter. Men have come to it in all ages,
full of a passionate desire to catch its meaning and
enter into its secret, but the thought of the bold-
est of them has only skirted its shores, and the vast
sweep of untamed waters remains as on the first
day. Homer has given us the song of the land-
locked sea, but where has the ocean found a human voice that is not lost and forgotten when it
speaks to us in its own penetrating tones ? The
mountains stand revealed in more than one interpretation, touched by their own sublimity, but the
sea remains silent in human speech, because no

voice will ever be strong enough to match its awful monody.

It is because the sea preserves its secret that it sways our imagination so royally, and holds us by an influence which never loosens its grasp. Again and again we return to it, spent and worn, and it refills the cup of vitality ; there is life enough and to spare in its invisible and inexhaustible chambers to reclothe the continents with verdure, and recreate the shattered strength of man. Facing its unbroken solitudes the limitations of habit and thought become less obvious ; we escape the monotony of a routine, which blurs the senses and makes the spirit less sensitive to the universe about it. Life becomes free and plastic once more ; a deep consciousness of its inexhaustibleness comes over us and recreates hope, vigor, and imagination. Under the little bridges of habit and theory, which we have made for ourselves, how vast and fathomless the sea of being is ! What undiscovered forces are there ; what unknown secrets of power ; what unsearchable possibilities of development and change ! How fresh and new becomes that which we thought outworn with use and touched with decay ! How boundless and untraveled that which we thought explored and sounded to its remotest bound !

At night, when the vision of the waters grows indistinct, what voices it has for our solitude ! The " eternal note of sadness," to which all ages and races have listened, and the faint echoes of which are heard in every literature, fills us with a longing as vast as the sea and as vague. Infinity and eternity are not too great for the spirit when the spell of the sea is on it, and the voice of the sea fills it with uncreated music.

CHAPTER IX.

A MOUNTAIN RIVULET.

THIS morning the day broke with a promise of sultry heat which has been faithfully kept. The air was lifeless, the birds silent; the landscape seemed to shrink from the ardor of a gaze that penetrated to the very roots of the trees, and covered itself with a faint haze. All things stood hushed and motionless in a dream of heat; even the harvest fields were deserted. On such a day nature herself becomes voiceless; she seems to retreat into those deep and silent chambers where the sources of her life are hidden alike from the heat and cold, from darkness and light. A strange and foreboding stillness is abroad in the earth, and one hides himself from the sun as from an enemy.

In this unnatural hush there was one voice which made the silence less ominous, and revived the spent and withered freshness of the spirit. To hear that voice seemed to me this morning the one consolation which the day offered. It called me with cool, delicious tones that seemed almost audible, and I braved the deadly heat as the traveler urges his way over the desert to the oasis that promises a draught of life. As I passed along the

A Mountain Rivulet

broad aisle of the village street, arched by the
venerable trees of an older generation, I seemed to
be in dreamland ; no sound broke the repose of
midday, no footstep echoed far or near ; the cattle
stood motionless in the fields beneath the shelter-
ing branches. I turned into the dusty country
road, and saw the vision of the great encircling
hills, remote, shadowless, and dreamlike, against
the white August sky. I sauntered slowly on,
pausing here and there at the foot of some sturdy
oak or wide-branched apple, until I reached the
little stream that comes rippling down from the
mountain glen. A short walk across the fields
under the burning sun brought me into the shadow
of the trees that skirt the borders of the woodland.
The brook loitered between its green and sloping
banks and broke in tiny billows over the smooth
stones that lay in its bed ; the shadows grew denser
as I advanced, and a delicious coolness from the
depths of the woods touched the sultry atmosphere.
A moment later, and I stood within the glen. The
world of human activity had vanished, shut out of
sight and sound by the deepening foliage of the
trees behind me. Overhead hardly a leaf stirred,
but the branching boughs spread a marvelous roof
between the heavens and the woodland paths, and
suffered only a stray flash of light here and there
to strike through. As I advanced slowly along the
well-worn path beside the brook, the glen grew
more and more narrow, the hillsides more and

more precipitous. In the dusky light that sifted
down through the great trees I felt the delicious re-
lief of low tones after the glare of the summer day.
It was another world into which I had come ; a
world of unbroken repose and silence, a world of
sweet and fragrant airs cooled by the mountain
rivulet and shielded by the mountain summits and
the arching umbrage.

The path vanished at last and nothing remained
but the narrow channel of the brook itself, the
smooth stones making a precarious and uncertain
footing for the adventurous explorer. How sooth-
ing was the ceaseless plash of that little stream,
fretting its moss-grown banks and dashing in miniature surge against the stones in its path ! What
infinite peace reigned in this place, around which
the brotherhood of mountains had gathered, to hold
it inviolate against all comers ! The great rocks
were moss-covered, the steep slopes on either side
were faintly flecked with light, and one saw here
and there, through the clustered trunks of trees, a
gleam of blue sky. Sometimes the brook narrowed
to a tiny stream, rushing with impetuous current
between the rocky walls that formed its channel ;
then it spread out shallow and noisy over some
broader expanse of white sand and polished pebble ;
then it loitered in the shadow of a great rock and
became a deep, silent pool, full of shadows and the
mysteries which lurk in such remote and dusky
places.

It was beside such a pool that I paused at last, and seated myself with infinite content. Before me the glen narrowed into a rocky chasm, over which the adventurous trees that clung to the precipitous hillsides spread a dense roof of foliage. The dark pool at my feet was full of mysterious shadows and seemed to cover epochs of buried history. As I studied its motionless surface the old medieval legends of black, fathomless pools came back to me, and I felt the air of enchantment stealing over me, lulling my latter-day skepticism into sleep, and making all mysteries rational and all marvels probable. In these silent depths no magical art had ever submerged cities or castles; on the stillest of all quiet afternoons no muffled echoes, faint and far, float up through the waveless waters. But who knows what shadows have sunk into these sunless depths; what reflections of waving branches, what siftings of subdued light, what hushed echoes of the forgotten summers that perished here ages ago?

In such a place, at such an hour, one feels the most subtle and the most searching spell which Nature ever throws over those that seek her; a spell woven of many charms, magical potions, and powerful incantations. The quiet of the place, awful with the unbroken silence of centuries; the soft, half light, which conceals more than it discloses; the retreating trunks of trees interlacing their branches against invasion from light or heat or sound ; the steep ravine, receding in darker and darker distance, until it seems like one of the fabled passages to the under world : the wide, shadowy pool, into which no sunlight falls, and in which night itself seems to sleep under the very eyes of day—all these things speak a language which even the dullest must understand.   As I sit musing, conscious of the darkest shadows and deepest mysteries close at hand, and yet undisturbed by them, I recall that one of the noblest poems on Death ever written was inspired in this place ; and I note without surprise, as its solemn lines come back to me, that there is no horror in it, no ignoble fear, but awe and reverence and the sublimity of a great and hopeful thought.   The organ music of those slow-moving verses seems like the very voice of a place out of which all dread has gone from the thought of death, and where the brief span of life seems to arch the abyss of death with immortality.

CHAPTER X.

THE EARLIEST INSIGHTS.

THE heaven which lies about us in our infancy, like every other heaven of which men have dreamed, lies mainly within us ; it is the heaven of fresh instincts, of unworn receptivity, of expanding intelligence. It is a heaven of faith and wonder, as every heaven must be ; it is a heaven of recurring miracle, of renewing freshness, of deepening interest. Into such a heaven every child is born who brings into life that leaven of the imagination which later on is to penetrate the universe and make it one in the sublime order of truth and of beauty.

As I write, the merry shouts of children come through the open window, and seem part of that universal sound in which the stir of leaves, the faint, far song of birds, and the note of insect life are blended. When I came across the field a few moments ago, a voice called me from under the apple trees, and a little figure, with a flush of joy on her face and the fadeless light of love in her eyes, came running with uneven pace to meet me. How slight and frail was that vision of childhood to the thought which saw the awful forces of nature at work, or rather at play, about her ! And yet how

51

serene was her look upon the great world dropping
its fruit at her feet ; how familiar and at ease her
attitude in the presence of these sublime mysteries !
She is at one with the hour and the scene ; she has
not begun to think of herself as apart from the
things which surround her ; that strange and sudden sense of unreality which makes me at times an
alien and a stranger in the presence of Nature,
" moving about in world not realized," is still far
off.   For her the sun shines and the winds blow,
the flowers bloom and the stars glisten, the trees
hold out their protecting arms and the grass
weaves its soft garment, and she accepts them
without a thought of what is behind them or shall
follow them ; the painful process of thought, which
is first to separate her from Nature and then to re-
unite her to it in a higher and more spiritual fellowship, has hardly begun.   She still walks in the
soft light of faith, and drinks in the immortal
beauty, as the flower at her side drinks in the dew
and the light.   It is she, after all, who is right as
she plays, joyously and at home, on the ground
which the earthquake may rock, and under the sky
which storms will darken and rend.   The far-
brought instinct of childhood accepts without a
question that great truth of unity and fellowship to
which knowledge comes only after long and agonizing quest.   Between the innocent sleep of childhood in the arms of Nature and the calm repose of
the old man in the same enfolding strength there

stretches the long, sleepless day of question, search, and suffering; at the end the wisest returns to the goal from which he set out.

To the little child, Nature is a succession of new and wonderful impressions. Coming he knows not whence, he opens his eyes upon a world which is as new to him as is the virgin continent to the first discoverer. It matters not that countless eyes have already opened and closed on the same magical appearances, that numberless feet have trodden the same paths; for him the morning star still shines on the first day, and the dew of the primeval night is still on the flowers. Day by day light and shadow fall in unbroken succession on the sensitive surface of his mind, and gradually an elementary order discovers itself in the regularity of these recurring impressions. Form, color, distance, size, relativity of position are felt rather than seen, and the dim and confused mass of sensations discovers something trustworthy and stable behind. Nature is now simple appearance; thought has not begun to inquire where the lantern is hidden which throws this wonderful picture on the clouds, nor who it is that shifts the scenes. Day and night alternately spread out a changeful successions of wonders simply that the young eyes may look upon them; and grass is green and sky blue that young feet may find soft resting-places and the young head a beautiful roof over it. Every day is a new discovery, and every night receives into its dreams some new object from the world of sights and sounds.

Nature surrounds her child with invisible teachers, and makes even its play a training for the highest duties. Gradually, imperceptibly, she expands the vision and suffers here and there a hint of something deeper and more wonderful to stir and direct the young discoverer. He sees the apple tree let fall its blossoms, and, lo! the fruit grows day by day to a mellow and enticing ripeness under his eyes. Suddenly he detects a hidden sequence between flower and fruit! The rose bush is covered with buds, small, green, unsightly; a night passes, and, behold! great clusters of blossoming flowers that call him by their fragrance, and when he has come reward him with a miracle of color. Here is another mystery; and day by day they multiply and grow yet more wonderful. These varied and marvelous appearances are no longer detached and changeless to him; they are alive, and they change moment by moment. Ah, the young feet have come now to the very threshold of the temple, and fortunate are they if there be one to guide them whose heart still speaks the language of childhood while her thought rests in the great truths which come with deep and earnest living. Childhood is defrauded of half its inheritance when no one swings wide before it the door into the fairyland of Nature; a land in which the most beautiful dreams are like visions of the distant Alps, cloudlike, apparently evanescent, yet eternally true ; in which the commonest realities are more wonderful than visions. How many children live all their childhood in the very heart of this realm, and are never so much as told to look about them. The sublime miracle play is yearly performed in their sight, and they only hear it said that it is hot or cold, that the day is fair or dark !

And now there come sudden insights into still larger and more awful truths ; a sense of wonder and awe makes the night solemn with mystery. Who does not recall some starlit night which suddenly, alone on a country road, perhaps, seemed to flash its splendor into his very soul and lift all life for a moment to a sublime height ? The trees stood silent down the long road, no other footstep echoed far or near, one was alone with Nature and at one with her ; suspecting no strange nearness of her presence, no sudden revelation of her inner self, and yet in the very mood in which these were both possible and natural. The boy of Wordsworth's imagination would stand beneath the trees " when the earliest stars began to move along the edges of the hills," and, with fingers interwoven, blow mimic hootings to the owls :

> And they would shout
> Across the watery vale, and shout again,
> Responsive to his call—with quivering peals,
> And long halloos, and screams, and echoes loud,

Redoubled and redoubled ; concourse wild
Of mirth and jocund din.   And when it chanced
That pauses of deep silence mock'd his skill,
Then, sometimes, in that silence, while he hung
Listening, a gentle shock of mild surprise
Has carried far into his heart the voice
Of mountain torrents ; or the visible scene
Would enter unawares into his mind
With all its solemn imagery, its rocks,
Its woods, and that uncertain heaven, received
Into the bosom of the steady lake.

It is in such moods as this, when all things are
forgotten, and heart and mind are open to every
sight and sound, that Nature comes to the soul
with some deep, sweet message of her inner being,
and with invisible hand lifts the curtain of mystery
for one hushed and fleeting moment.

As I write, the memory of a summer afternoon
long ago comes back to me. The old orchard
sleeps in the dreamy air, the birds are silent, a tranquil spirit broods over the whole earth. Under the
wide-spreading branches a boy is intently reading.
He has fallen upon a bit of transcendental writing
in a magazine, and for the first time has learned
that to some men the great silent world about him,
that seems so real and changeless, is immaterial
and unsubstantial—a vision projected by the soul
upon illimitable space. On the instant all things
are smitten with unreality ; the solid earth sinks
beneath him, and leaves him solitary and awestruck
in a universe that is a dream. He cannot under-

stand, but he feels what Emerson meant when he said, " The Supreme Being does not build up Nature around us, but puts it forth through us, as the life of the tree puts forth new branches and leaves." That which was fixed, stable, cast in permanent forms forever, was suddenly annihilated by a revelation which spoke to the heart rather than the intellect, and laid bare at a glance the unseen spiritual foundations upon which all things rest at last. From that moment the boy saw with other eyes, and lived henceforth in things not made with hands.

If we could but revive the consciousness of childhood, if we could but look out once more through its unclouded eyes, what divinity would sow the universe with light and make it radiant with fadeless visions of beauty and of truth !

pears, and I am breathing the universal life ; I have gone back to the far beginning of things, and I am once more in that dim, rich moment of primeval contact with Nature out of which all mythologies and literatures have grown. How profound and all-embracing is the silence, and yet how full of inarticulate sound ! The faint whisperings of the leaves touch me first with a sense of melody, and then, later, with a sense of mystery. These are the most venerable voices to which men have ever listened ; and when I think of the immeasurable life that seems to be groping for utterance in them, I remember with no consciousness of skepticism that these are the voices which men once waited upon as oracles ; nay, rather, wait upon still ; for am I not now listening for the word which shall speak to me out of these shadowy depths and this mysterious antique life ? I am ready to listen and to follow if only these vagrant sounds shall blend into one clear note and declare to me that secret which they have kept so well through the centuries. I wait expectant, as I have waited so often before ; there is unbroken stillness, then a faint murmur slowly rising and spreading until I am sure that the moment of revelation has come, then a slow recession back to silence. I am not discouraged ; sooner or later that multitudinous rustle of the wild woods will break into clear-voiced speech. I am sure, too, that some great movement of life is about to display itself before me. Is not this hush the sudden stillness of those whom I have surprised and who have, on the instant, sprung to their coverts and are waiting impatiently until I have gone, to resume their interrupted frolic! I have often watched and waited here before in vain, but surely to-day I shall beguile these hidden folk into revelation of that wonderful life they have suddenly suspended! So I throw myself at the foot of a great pine, and wait; the minutes move slowly across the unseen dial of the day, and I have become so still and motionless that I am part of this secluded world. The sun shines abroad, but I have forgotten it; there are clouds passing all day in their aerial journeyings, but they cast no shadow over me; even the flight of the hours is unnoticed. Eternity might come and I should be no wiser, I should see no change; for does it not already hold these vast dim aisles and solitudes within its peaceful empire? And is there not here the slow procession of birth, decay, and death, in that sublime order of growth which we call immortality?

I wait and watch, and I can wait forever if need be. Suddenly from the depths of the forest there comes a note of penetrating sweetness, wild, magical, ethereal; I slowly raise myself and wait. Surely this is the signal, and in a moment I shall see the dim spaces between the trees peopled and animate. There is a moment's pause, and then again that strange, mysterious song rings through the listening forest. It touches me like a sudden

revelation ; I forget that for which I have waited ;
I only know that the woods have found their voice,
and that I have fallen upon the sacred hour when
the song is a prayer. Who shall describe that wild,
strange music of the hermit-thrush ? Who will
ever hear it in the depths of the forest without a
sudden thrill of joy and a sudden sense of pathos ?
It is a note apart from the symphony to which the
summer has moved across the fields and homes of
men ; it has no kinship with those flooding, liquid
melodies which poured from feathered throats
through the long golden days ; there is a strain in
it that was never caught under blue skies and in
the safe nesting of the familiar fields ; it is the
voice of solitude suddenly breaking into sound ; it
is the speech of that other world so near our doors,
and yet removed from us by uncounted centuries
and unexplored experiences.

The spell of silence has been broken, and I venture softly toward the hidden fountain from which
this unworldly song has flowed ; but I am too slow
and too late, and it remains to me a disembodied
voice singing the "old, familiar things" of a past
which becomes more and more distinct as I linger
in the shadows of this ancient place. As I walk
slowly on, there grows upon me the sense of a life
which for the most part makes no sound, and is all
the deeper and richer because it is inarticulate.
The very thought of speech or companionship jars
upon me ; silence alone is possible for such hours

and moods. The great movement of life which builds these mighty trunks and sends the vital currents to their highest branches, which alternately clothes and denudes them, makes no sound ; cycle after cycle have the completed centuries made, and yet no sign of waning power here, no evidence of a finished work ! Here life first dawned upon men ; here, slowly, it discovered its meaning to them ; here the first impressions fell upon senses keen with desire for untried sensations ; here the first great thoughts, vast as the forest and as shadowy, moved slowly on toward conscious clearness in minds that were just beginning to think ; here and not elsewhere are the roots of those earliest conceptions of Nature and Life, which again and again have come to such glorious blossoming in the literatures of the race. This is, in a word, the world of primal instinct and impression ; and, therefore, forever the deepest, most familiar, and yet most marvelous world to which men may come in all their wanderings.

As these thoughts come and go, unclothed with words and unsought by will, I grasp again the deep truth that the truest life is unconscious and almost voiceless ; that there is no rich, true, articulate life unless there flows under it a wide, deep current of unspoken, almost unconscious, thought and feeling; that the best one ever says or does is as a few drops flung into the sunlight from a swift, hidden stream, and shining for a moment as they fall again into a current inaudible and invisible. The intellectual life that is all expressed, that is all conscious and self-directed, is but a shallow life at best ; he only lives deeply in the intellect whose thought begins in instinct, rises slowly through experience, carrying with it into consciousness the noblest, truest one has felt and been, and finds speech at last by impulse and direction of the same law which summons the seed from the soil and lifts it, growth by growth, to the beauty and the sweetness of the flower. Under the same law of unconscious growth every true poem, every great work of art, and every genuine noble character, has fashioned itself and come at last to conscious perfectness and recognition. Genius is nearer Nature than talent ; it is only when it strays away from Nature, and loses itself in mere dexterities, that it degenerates into skill and becomes a tool with which to work, and not a gift from heaven. The silence of the deep woods is pregnant with mighty growths. Says Maurice de Guérin, true poet and lover of Nature : " An innumerable generation actually hangs on the branches of all the trees, on the fibers of the most insignificant grasses, like babes on the mother's breast. All these germs, incalculable in their number and variety, are there suspended in their cradle between heaven and earth, and given over to the winds, whose charge it is to rock these beings. Unseen amid the living forests swing the forests of the future.

Nature is all absorbed in the vast cares of her maternity."

But while I walk and meditate, letting the forest tell its story to my innermost thought, and recalling here only that which is most obvious and superficial (who is sufficient for the deeper things that lie like pearls in the depths of his being ?), the light grows dimmer, and I know that the day has gone. I re-trace my steps until through the clustered trunks of the trees I see once more the green meadows soft in the light of sunset. As I pass over the boundary line of the forest once more, faint and far the song of the thrush searches the wood, and, finding me, leaves its ethereal note in my memory— a note wild as the forest, and thrilling into momen-tary consciousness I know not what forgotten ages of awe and wonder and worship.

CHAPTER XII

BESIDE THE RIVER.

ALL day long the river has moved through my thought as it rolls through the landscape spread out at my feet. There it lies, winding for many a mile within the boundaries of this noble outlook; by day flecked with sails approaching and receding, and at night shining under the full moon like a girdle of silver, clasping mountains and broad meadow lands in a varied but harmonious landscape. From the point at which I look out upon its long course, the stream has a setting worthy of its volume and its history. In the distant background a mountain range, of noble altitude and outline, has to-day an ethereal strength and splendor; a slight haze has obliterated all details, and left the great hills soft and dreamlike in the September sunshine; at first sight one waits to see them vanish, but they remain, wrought upon by sunlight and atmosphere, until the twilight touches them with purple and night turns them into mighty shadows. On either hand, in the middle ground of the picture, long lines of hills shut the river within a world of its own, and shelter the green meadows, the fallow fields, and the stretches of woodland that cover the broad sweep from the river's edge to their own bases. Below me the quiet current enters the heart of another group of mountains, flowing silently between the precipitous and rocky heights that lift themselves on either hand, indifferent alike to the frowning summits when the sun warms them with smiles, and to the black and portentous shadows which they often cast across the channel at their feet. The solitude and awe which belong to mountain passes through which great rivers flow clothe this place with solemnity and majesty as with a visible garment, and fill one with a sense of indescribable awe.

The river which lies before me moves through a mist of legend and tradition as well as through a landscape of substantial history. It has been called an epical river because of the varied and sustained beauty through which it sweeps from its mountain sources to the sea; but as I turn from it, and the visible loveliness of its banks fades from sight, I recall that other landscape of history and legend through which it rolls, and that, for the moment, is the reality, and the other the shadow. A web of human associations spreads itself over this long valley like a richer atmosphere; the fields are ripe with action and achievement; every projecting point has its story, every gentle curve and quiet inlet its memory; for many and many a decade of years life has touched this silent stream and humanized its power and beauty until it has become part

of the vast human experience wrought out between
these mountain boundaries. As I think of these
things and of the world of dear past things which
they recall, another great river sweeps into the
vision of memory, but how different !   There comes
with it no warmth of human emotion, but only the
breath of the unbroken woods, the awful aspect of
the great, precipitous cliffs, the vast solitude out of
which it rolls, with troubled current, to mingle its
mysterious waters with the northern gulf.   It is a
stream which Nature still keeps for herself, and
suffers no division of ownership with men; a stream
as wild and solitary as the remote and unpeopled
land through which it moves.   This river, on the
other hand, bears every hour the wealth of a great
inland commerce upon its wide current ; it flows
past cities and villages scattered thickly along its
course, past countless homes whose lights weave a
shining net along its banks at night; on still Sabbath mornings the bells answer each other in almost
unbroken peal along its course.   Emerging from
an unknown past in the earliest days of discovery,
human interests have steadily multiplied along its
shores, and spread over it the countless lines of
human activity.   To-day the Argo, multiplied a
thousand times, seeks the golden fleece of commerce at every point along its shores ; and of the
countless Jasons who make the voyage few return
empty-handed.   Hour after hour the white sails fly
in mysterious and changing lines, messengers of

wealth and trade and pleasure, whose voyages are no sooner ended than they begin again. It is this wealth of action and achievement which make the names of great rivers sonorous as the voices of the centuries ; the Nile, the Danube, the Rhine, the Hudson—how weighty are these words with associations old as history and deep as the human heart !

The rivers are the great channels through which the ceaseless interchange of the elements goes on ; they unite the heart of the continents and the solitary places of the mountains with the universal sea which washes all shores and beats its melancholy refrain at either pole. Into their currents the hills and uplands pour their streams ; to them the little rivulets come laughing and singing down from their sources in the forest depths. A drop falling from a passing shower into the lake of Delolo may be carried eastward, through the Zambesi, to the Indian Ocean, or westward, along the transcontinental course of the Congo, to the Atlantic. The mists that rise from great streams, separated by vast stretches of territory, commingle in the upper air, and are carried by vagrant winds to the wheat-fields of the far Northwest or the rice-fields of the South. The ocean ceaselessly makes the circuit of the globe, and summons its tributaries along all shores to itself. But it gives even more lavishly than it receives; day and night there rise over its vast expanse those invisible clouds of moisture which dif-

fuse themselves through the atmosphere, and descend at last upon the earth to pour, sooner or later, into the rivers, and be returned whence they came. This subtle commerce, universal throughout the whole domain of nature, animate and inanimate, tells us a common truth with the rose, and corrects the false report of the senses that all things are fixed and isolated. It discloses a communion of matter with matter, a fellowship of continent with continent, an interchange of forces which throws a broad light on things still deeper and more marvelous. It affirms the unity of all created things and predicts the dawn of a new thought of the kinship of races; there is in it the prophecy of new insights into the universal life of men, of fellowships that shall rise to the recognition of new duties, and of a well-being which shall bind the weakest to the strongest, the poorest to the richest, the lowest to the highest, by the golden bond of a diviner love.

CHAPTER XIII.

AT THE SPRING.

THE path across the fields is so well worn that one can find his way along its devious course by night almost as easily as by day. I have gone over it at all hours, and have never returned without some fresh and cheering memory for other and less favored days. The fields across which it leads one, with the unfailing suggestion of something better beyond, are undulating and dotted here and there with browsing cattle. The landscape is full of pastoral repose and charm—the charm of familiar things that are touched with old memories, and upon whose natural beauty there rests the reflected light of days that have become idyllic. No one can walk along a country road, over which as a boy he heard the daily invitation of the schoolhouse bell without discovering at every turn some loveliness never revealed save to the glance of unforgotten youth. The path which leads to the spring has this unfailing charm for me, and for many who have long ceased to follow its winding course. At this season it is touched here and there by the autumnal splendor, and fairly riots in the profusion of the golden-rod, whose yellow plumes are lighting the retreating steps of summer across the fields. Great masses of brilliant woodbine cover the stone walls and hang from the trees along the fences. The corn, cut and stacked in orderly lines, is not without its transforming touch of color; and while the trees still wait for the coronation of the year Nature seems to have passed along this path and turned it into a royal highway. As it approaches the woods, one gets glimpses of the village spires in the distance, and find a new charm in this border-land between sunlight and shadow, between solitude and the companionship of human life. A little distance along the edges of the woods, with an occasional detour of the path into the shades of the forest, brings one to the spring. A great, rudely-cut stone marks the place, and makes a kind of background for the cool, limpid pool into which a few leaves fall from the woods, but which belongs to the open sky and fields. There is certainly no more gentle, reposeful scene than this; so secluded from the dust and whirl of cities and thoroughfares, and yet so near to ancient homes, so sweet and life-giving in its service to them, so often and so eagerly sought at all seasons and by men of all conditions. Here oftenest come the restless feet of children, and their shouts are almost the only sounds that ever break this solitude.

To me there is something inexpressibly sweet and refreshing in the familiar and yet unfailing loveliness of this place. The fields are always peaceful, and the slow motions of the cattle grouped here and there under the shadows of solitary trees, or of the sheep browsing in long, irregular lines across the further meadows, give the landscape that touch of pastoral life which unites us with Nature in the oldest and most homelike relations. Here, on still summer afternoons, one seems to have come upon a sleeping world; a world over whose slumber the clouds are passing like peaceful dreams. In such an hour the limpid water of the spring seems to rise out of the very heart of the earth, and to bring with it an unfailing refreshment of spirit. The white sand through which it finds its way makes its transparent clearness more apparent, and the great stone seems to hold back the woods from an approach that would overshadow it. It rises so silently into the visible world from the unseen depths that one cannot but feel some illusion of sentiment thrown over it, some disclosure of truth escaping with it from the darkness beneath. Whence does it flow, and what has its journey been? Did some remote mountain range gather its waters from the clouds and send them down through long and winding channels deep in its heart? Is there far below an invisible stream flowing, like the river Alphæus, unseen and unheard beneath the earth? The spring is mute when these questions rise to lips which it is always ready to moisten from its cool depths. It is

enough that in this quiet place the bounty of
Nature never ceases to overflow, and that here she
holds out the cup of refreshment with royal indifference to gratitude or neglect.   Here she ministers
to every comer as if her whole life were a service.
One forgets that behind this cup of cold water, held
out to the humblest, there sweep sublime powers,
and that the same hand which serves him here
moves in their courses the planets, whose faint reflections shine in this silent pool by night.

Springs have been natural centers of life from the
earliest times.   Deep in the solitude of forests, or
fringed with foliage in the heart of deserts, they
have alike served the needs and appealed to the
sentiment of men.   Around the wells cluster the
most venerable associations of the ancient patri-
archal families ; the beautiful pastoral life of the
Old Testament, full of deep, unwritten poetry, discovers no scenes more characteristic and touching
than those which were enacted beside these sources
of fertility.   Green and fruitful in the memory of
the most sacred history repose these cool, refreshing pools under the burning glance of the tropical
sun.   Here, too, as in those distant lands, life is
kept in constant freshness around the borders of
the spring.   The grass grows green and dense here
the whole summer through, and here there is always
a breath of cooler air when the fields glow with intense heat.   In such places Nature waits to touch

the fevered spirit with something of her own peace, and to keep alive forever in the hearts of men that faith in things unseen which rises like a spring from the depths, and makes a center of fruitful and beautiful life.

CHAPTER XIV.

NATURE creates days for special insights and outlooks—days whose distinctive qualities make them part of the universal revelation of the year. There are days for the deep woods, and for the open fields ; days for the beach, and for the inland river ; days for solitary musing beside some secluded rivulet, and days for the companionship and movement of the highways. Each day is fitted by some subtle magic of adaptation to the place and the aspect of nature which it is to reveal with a clearness denied to other hours. There came such a day not long ago to me ; a day of tonic atmosphere—clear, cloudless, inspiring ; there was no audible invitation in the air, but I knew by some instinct that the day and the mountains were parts of one complete whole. The morning itself was a new birth of nature, full of promise and prophecy ; one of those hours in which only the greatest and noblest things are credible, in which one rejects unfaith and doubt and all lesser and meaner things as dreams of a night from which there has come an eternal awakening ; a day such as Emerson had in thought when he wrote : " The

76

scholar must look long for the right hour for Plato's Timæus. At last the elect morning arrives, the early dawn—a few lights conspicuous in the heaven, as of a world just created and still becoming—and in its wide leisure we dare open that book. There are days when the great are near us, when there is no frown on their brow, no condescension even ; when they take us by the hand, and we share their thought." When such a morning dawns, one demands, by right of his own nature, the pilotage of great thoughts to some height whence the whole world will lie before him ; one knows by unclouded insight that life is greater than all his dreams, and that he is heir, not only of the centuries, but of eternity.

Such days belong to the mountains; and when I opened my window on this morning, I was in no doubt as to the invitation held forth by earth and sky. There was exhilaration in the very thought of the long climb, and at an early hour I was fast leaving the village behind me. The road skirted the base of the mountain, and struck at once into the heart of the wilderness, which the clustering peaks have preserved from any but the most fleeting associations with the peopled world around. A barrier of ancient silence and solitude soon separated me even in thought from the familiar scenes I had left. A virginal beauty rested upon the road, and sank deep into my own heart as I passed along ; to be silent and open-minded was enough to bring one into fellowship with the hour and the scene. ⟩The clear, bracing air, the rustling of leaves slowly sifting down through the lower branches, the solemn quietude, filled the morning with a deep joy that touched the very sources of life, and made them sweet in every thought and emotion. It was like a new beginning in the old, old story of time ; the stains of ancient wrong, the blights of sorrow, the wrecks of hope, were gone ; sweet with the untrod-den freshness of a new day lay the earth, and looked up to the heavens with a gaze as pure and calm as their own. Somehow all life seemed sub-limated in that golden sunshine ;⟨ the grosser elements had vanished, the material had become the transparent medium of the spiritual, the dis-cords had blended into harmony, and one would have heard without surprise the faint, far song of the stars. The whole world was one vast articulate poem, and human life added its own strain of pene-trating sweetness.⟩ At last, after all these years of struggle and failure, one was really living !

⟨The road, slowly ascending the long wooded slope, wound its way through the forest until it brought me to the mountain path which climbs, with many a halt and pause, to the very summit. Dense foliage overshadows it, a little thinner now that the hand of autumn has begun to disrobe the trees. Great rocks often lie in the course of the path and send it in a narrow curve around them. Sometimes one comes upon a bold ascent up the

face of a projecting cliff ; sometimes one plunges
into the very heart of the shadows as they gather
over the rocky channel of the brook that later will
run foaming down to the valley. Step by step one
widens his horizon, although it is only at intervals
that he is able to note his progress upward.) At
the base of the mountain one saw only a circle of
hills, and the long sweep of wooded slopes which
converge in the valley ; gradually the horizon
widens as one climbs beyond the summit lines of
the lower hills ; at turns in the path, where it
crosses some rocky declivity, one looks out upon a
landscape into which some new feature enters with
every new outlook; one range of hills after another
sinks below the level of vision, and discloses another
strip of undiscovered country beyond ; and so one
climbs, step by step, into the glory of a new world.
The solitude, the silence, the radiant beauty of the
morning, the expanding sweep of hills and valleys
at one's feet, fill one with eager longing for the unbroken circle of sky at the summit, and prepare one
for the thrill of joy with which the soul answers
the outspread vision.

At last only a few rocks interpose between the
summit and the last resting-place. I wait a moment longer than I need, as one pushes back for
an instant the cup from which he has long desired
to drink. I even shun the noble vistas that open
on either side, postponing to the moment of perfect
achievement the partial successes already won.

But the rocks are soon climbed, the summit is reached! The world is at my feet—the mountain ranges like great billows, and the valleys, deep, far, and shadowy, between; and overhead the unbroken arch of sky melting into illimitable space through infinite gradations of blue. The vision which has haunted me so long with illusive hints of range and splendor is mine at last, and I have no greeting for it but the breathless eagerness with which I turn from point to point, as if to drink all in with one compelling glance. But the landscape does not yield its infinite variety to the first nor to the second glance; the agitation of the first outlook gives place to a deep, calm joy; the eager desire to possess on the instant what has been won by long toil and patience is followed by a quiet mood which banishes all thought of self, and waits upon the hour and the scene for the revelation they will make in their own good time. Slowly the noble landscape reveals itself to me in its vast range and its marvelous variety. The somber groups of mountains to the west become distinct and majestic as I look into their deep recesses; far off to the north the massive bulk and impressive outlines of a solitary peak grow upon me until it seems to dominate the whole country-side. A kingly mountain truly, of whose "night of pines" our saintly poet has sung; from this distance a vast and softened shadow against the stainless sky. To the east one sees the long uplands, with slender spires rising here and there from clustered homes; to the south, a vast stretch of fertile fields, rolling like a fruitful sea to the horizon; within the mighty circle, groups of lower hills, wooded valleys shadowy and mysterious in the distance, villages and scattered homes.

It was a deep saying of Goethe's that " on every height there lies repose." (A Sabbath stillness and solemnity reign in this upper sphere, where the sound of human toil never comes and the cry of humanity never penetrates. The boundaries that confine and baffle the vision along the walks of ordinary life have all faded out; great States lie together in this outlook without visible lines of division or separation. The obstacles to sight which hourly baffle and confuse are gone; from horizon to horizon all things are clear and visible, and the world is vast and beautiful to its remotest boundaries.) The repose which lies on the heights of life is born of the vast and unclouded vision which looks down upon all obstacles, over all barriers, and takes in at a glance the mighty scope of human activity and the unbroken sky which overhangs it continually like a visible infinity. On such heights it is the blessed reward of a few elect souls to live; but the paths thither are open to every traveler.

CHAPTER XV.

UNDER COLLEGE ELMS.

STRETCHED under the spreading branches of this noble elm, which has seen so many college generations come and go, I have well-nigh forgotten that life has any limitations of space or time ; work, anxiety, weariness fade out of thought under a heaven from which every cloud has vanished, and the eye pierces everywhere the infinite depths of the upper firmament. Days are not always radiant here, and the stream of life as it flows through this tranquil valley is flecked with shadows ; but all sweet influences have combined to touch this passing hour with unspeakable peace. Here are the old familiar footpaths trodden so often with hurrying feet in other years ; here are the well-worn seats about which familiar groups have so often gathered and sent the echoes of their songs flying heavenward ; here are the rooms which will never lose the sense of home because of those who have lived in them. The chapel bell tolls as of old, and the crowd comes hurrying along like the generations before them, but the eye sees no familiar faces among them. It is a place of intense and rich living, and yet to-day, and for me, it is a place of memory. The life once lived here is as truly finished as if eternity had placed the impassable gulf between it and this quiet hour. These are the shores through which the river once passed, these the green fields which encircled it, these the mountains which flung their shadows over it, but the river itself has swept leagues onward.

Mr. Higginson has written charmingly about " An Old Latin Text-Book," and there is surely something magical in the power with which these well-worn volumes lay their spell upon us, and carry us back to other scenes and men. I have a copy of Virgil from which all manner of old-time things slip out as I open its pages. The eager enthusiasm of the first dawning appreciation of the undying beauty of the old poet, faintly discerned in the language which embalms it, comes back like a whiff of fragrance from some by-gone summer. The potency of college memories lies in the fact that in those years we made the most memorable discoveries of our lives ; the unknown river may widen and deepen beyond our thought, but the most noteworthy moment in all our wanderings with it will always be the moment when we first came upon it, and there dawned upon us the sense of something new and great. To most boys this rich and never-to-be-forgotten experience comes in college. Except in cases of rare good fortune, a boy is not ripe for the literary spirit in the classic literature until the college atmosphere surrounds him. To many it never discovers itself at all, and the languages which were dead at the beginning of study are dead at the end ; but to those in whom the instinct of scholarship is developed there comes a day when Virgil lives as truly as he lived in Dante's imagination, and, like Boccaccio, they light a fire at his tomb which years do not quench.

Who that has ever gone through the experience will forget the hour when he discovered the Greeks in Homer's pages, and felt for the first time the grand impulse of that noble race stir his blood and fill his brain with the far-reaching aspiration for a life as rich as theirs in beauty, freedom, and strength ! It is told of an English scholar that he devoted his winters to the "Iliad" and his summers to the "Odyssey," reading each several times every year. One could hardly reconcile such self-indulgence with the claims of to-day on every man's time and strength ; but I have no doubt all Grecians have a secret envy for such a career. The Old-World charm of the "Odyssey" is one of the priceless possessions of every fresh student, and to feel it for the first time is like discovering the sea anew. It is, indeed, the Epic of the Sea ; the only poem in all literature which gives the breadth, the movement, the mighty sweep of sky belted with stars, the unspeakable splendors of sunrise and sunset,—the grand, free life of the sea. I would place the "Odyssey" in every collection of modern books for the tonic quality that is in it.

The dash of wave and the roar of wind play havoc with our melancholy, and fill us with shame that we have so much as asked the question, " Is Life Worth Living ? "

There is no grander entrance gate to the great world of thought than the Greek Literature. Universities are broadening their courses to meet the multiplied demands of modern knowledge and to fit men for the varied pursuits of modern life, but for those who desire familiarity with human life in its broadest expression, and especially for those who seek familiarity with the literary spirit and mastery of the literary art, Greek must hold its place in the curriculum to the end of time. This implies no disparagement of our own literature—a literature which spreads its dome over a wider world of feeling and knowledge than the Greek ever saw within the horizon of his experience ; but the Greek, like the Hebrew, will remain to the latest generation among the great teachers of men. He was born into the first rank among nations ; he had an eye quick to see, a mind clear, open, and bold to grasp facts, set them in order, and generalize their law ; an instinct for art that turned all his observation and thinking into literature. Whether he looked at the world about him or fixed his gaze upon his own nature, his insight was from the very beginning so direct, so commanding, so perfectly allied with beauty, that his speculations became philosophy and his emotions poetry. There was hardly any aspect of life which he did not see, no question which he did not ask, and few which he failed to answer with more or less of truth. He walked through an untrodden world of sights and sounds, and reproduced the vast circle of his life in a literature to which men will look as long as the world stands for models of sweetness, beauty, and power. Greek literature holds its place, not because scholars have combined to keep alive its traditions and make familiarity with it the bond of the fellowship of culture, but because it is the faithful reflection of the life of a race who faced the world on all sides with masterly intelligence and power. It is a liberal education to have traveled from Æschylus, with his almost Asiatic splendor of imagination, to Theocritus, under whose exquisite touch the soft outlines of Sicilian life took on idyllic loveliness!

And then there were those unbroken winter evenings, when one began really to know the great modern masters of literature. What would one not give to have them back again, with their undisturbed hours ending only when the fire or the lamp gave out! Those were nights of royal fellowships, of introduction into the noblest society the world has ever known, and it is the recollection of this companionship which gives those days under college roofs a unique and perennial charm. Then first the spirit of our own race was revealed to us in Chaucer, Shakespeare, and Milton; then first we

thrilled to that music which has never faltered
since Cædmon found his voice in answer to the
heavenly vision. There are days which will always
have a place by themselves in our memory, nights
whose stars have never set, because they brought
us face to face with some great soul, and struck
into life in an instant some new and mighty meaning. The ferment of soul which Hazlitt describes
on the night when he walked home from his first
talk with Coleridge is no exceptional experience ;
it comes to most young men who are susceptible to
the influence of great thoughts coming for the first
time into consciousness. A lonely country road
comes into view as I write these words, and over
it the heavens bend with a new and marvelous
splendor, because the boy who walked along its
winding course had just finished for the first time,
and in a perfect tumult of soul, Schiller's " Rob-
bers "; it was the power of a great master, felt
through his crudest work, that filled the night with
such magical influences.

The hours in which we come in contact with
great souls are always memorable in our history,
often the crises in our intellectual life ; it is the
recollection of such hours that gives those bending
elms an imperishable charm, and lends to this landscape a deathless interest.

CHAPTER XVI.

A SUMMER MORNING.

I DO not understand how any one who has watched the breaking of a summer day can question the noblest faiths of man. William Blake, with that integrity of insight which is often the possession of the true mystic, declared that when he was asked if he saw anything more in a sunset than a round disk of fire, he could only answer that he saw an innumerable company of the heavenly host crying " Holy, Holy, Holy Lord God Almighty ! " The birth of a day is a diviner miracle even than its death. They were true poets who wrote the old Vedic hymns and sang those wonderful adorations when the last stars were fading in the splendor of the dawn. Beside the glory of the sun's announcement all royal progresses are tawdry and mean ; beside the beauty of the dawn, slowly unveiling the day while the heavens wait in silent worship, all poetry is idle and empty. It is the divinest of all the visible processes of nature, and the sublimest of all her marvelous symbolism.

On such a morning as this, twelve years ago, Amiel wrote in his diary : " The whole atmosphere has a luminous serenity, a limpid clearness. The

islands are like swans swimming in a golden stream.
Peace, splendor, boundless space ! . . . . I long to
catch the wild bird, happiness, and tame it. These
mornings impress me indescribably. They intoxi-
cate me, they carry me away. I feel beguiled out
of myself, dissolved in sunbeams, breezes, perfumes,
and sudden impulses of joy. And yet all the time
I pine for I know not what intangible Eden." In
these few words this master of poetic meditation
suggests without expressing the indescribable impression which a summer carries into every sensitive nature.

Last night the world was sorrowful, worn, and
dulled ; but lo ! the new day has but touched it
and all the invisible choirs are heard again ; the
old hope returns like a tide, and out of the unseen
depths a new life breaks soundless upon the unseen
shores and sends its hidden currents into every
dried and empty channel and pool. The worn old
world has been created anew, and God has spoken
again the word out of which all living things grow.
In the silence and peace and freshness of this
morning hour one feels the inspiration of nature as
a direct and personal gift ; the inbreathing, which
has renewed the beauty and fertility about him,
renews his spirit also. He responds to the fresh
and invigorating atmosphere with a soul sensitive
with sudden return of zest to every beautiful sight
and sound. No longer an alien in this world which
has never known human care and regret, he enters

by right of citizenship into all its privileges of un-
watched freedom and unclouded serenity. One is
not absorbed by the glory of the morning, but set
free by it. There are times when Nature permits
no rivalry; she claims every thought and gives
herself to us only as we give ourselves to her.
She effaces us and takes complete possession of
our souls. Not so, however, does she usurp the
throne of our own personal life in those early
hours when the sun, the master artist, whose touch
has colored every leaf and tinted every flower,
demands her adoration. Then it is, perhaps, that
she turns her thoughts from all lesser companionships and, rapt in universal worship, suffers us to
pass and repass as unnoticed as the idlers in the
cathedral by those who kneel at the chancel rail.

I confess I never find myself quite unmoved in
this sacred hour, announced only by the stars veiling their faces and the birds breaking the silence
with their tumultuous song. The universal faith
becomes mine also, and from the common worship
I am not debarred. My thought rises whither the
mists, parted from the unseen censers, are rising:
I feel within me the revival of aspirations and faiths
that were fast overclouding; the stir of old hopes
is in my heart; the thrill of old purposes is in my
soul. Once more Nature is serving me in an hour
of need; serving me not by drawing me to herself,
but by setting me free from a world that was beginning to master and make me its slave.

Now all that insensibly growing servitude slips from me ; once more I am free and my own. The inexhaustible life that is ·behind all visible things, constantly flowing in upon us when we keep the channels open, recreates whatever was noblest and truest in me. With Nature, I believe ; and believing, I also share in the universal worship.

Emerson somewhere says, writing about the most difficult of Plato's dialogues, that one must often wait long for the hour when one is strong enough to grapple with and master it, but sooner or later the fitting morning will come. It is the morning which gives us faith in the most arduous achievements, and invigorates us to undertake them. In the morning all things are possible because the heavens and the earth are so visibly united in the fellowship of common life ; the one pouring down a measureless and penetrating tide of vitality, the other eagerly, worshipfully receptive. Nature has no more inspiring truth for us than this constant and complete enfolding of our life by a higher and vaster life, this unbroken play of a diviner purpose and force through us. Nothing is lost, nothing really dies ; all things are conserved by an energy which transforms, reorganizes, and perpetuates in new and finer forms all visible things. The silence of winter counterfeits the repose of death, but it is not even a pause of life ; invisibly to us the great movement goes on in the earth under our feet. While we watch by our household fires, the unseen

architects are planning the summer, and the sublime march of the stars is noiselessly bringing back
the bloom and the perfume that seem to have vanished forever. Every morning restores something
we thought lost, recalls some charm that seemed to
have escaped.

In all noble natures there is an ineradicable
idealism which constantly interprets life in its
higher aspects. In the dust of the road the mountains sometimes disappear from our vision, but we
know that they still loom in undiminished majesty
against the horizon ; the gods sometimes hide
themselves, but there is something within which
affirms that we shall again look on their serene
faces, calm amid our turbulence and unchanging
amid our vicissitudes. It is this heavenly inheritance of insight and faith which makes Nature so
divinely significant to us, and matches all its forms
and phenomena with spiritual realities not to be
taken from us by time or change or by that mysterious angel of the last great transformation which
we call death. The morning is always breaking
over the low horizon lines of some sea or continent ; voices of birds are always "caroling against
the gates of day " ; and so, through unbroken
light and song, our life is solemnly and sublimely
moved onward to the dawn in which all the faint
stars of our hope shall melt into the eternal day.

CHAPTER XVII.

A SUMMER NOON.

THE stir of the morning has given place to a silence broken only by the shrill whir of the locust. The distant shore lines that ran clear and white against the low background of green have become dim and indistinct; all things are touched by a soft haze which changes the sentiment of the landscape from movement to repose, from swift and multitudinous activity to the hush of sleep. The intense blue of the morning sky is dimmed and the great masses of trees are motionless. The distant harvest fields where the rhythmic lines of the mowers have moved alert and harmonious through the morning hours are deserted. On earth silence and rest, and in the great arch of the sky a sea of light so full and splendid that it seems almost to dim the fiery effluence of the sun itself. In such an hour one stretches himself under the trees, and in a moment the spell is on him, and he cares neither to think nor act; he rejoices to lose himself in the universal repose with which Nature refreshes herself. The heat of the day is at its height, but for an hour the burden slips from the

shoulders of care, and the rest comes in which the
gains of work are garnered.

The whir of the locust high overhead, by some
earlier association, always recalls that matchless
singer, some of whose notes Nature has never
regained in all these later years.   The whir of the
cicada and the white light on the remote country
road are real to us to-day, though one went silent
and the other faded out of Sicilian skies two thousand years and more ago, because both are preserved in the verse of Theocritus.   The poet was
something more than a mere observer of Nature,
and the beautiful repose of his art more than the
native grace and ease of one to whom life meant
nothing more strenuous than a dream of a blue sea
and fair sky.   He had known the din of the
crowded street as well as the silence of the country
road, the forms and shows of a royal court as well
as the simplicity and sincerity of tangled vines and
gnarled olives on the hillside.   He had seen, with
those eyes which overlooked nothing, the pomps
and vanities of power, the fret and fever of
ambition, the impotence and barrenness of much of
that activity in which multitudes of men spend their
lives under the delusion that mere stir and bustle
mean progress and achievement.   Out of Syracuse,
with its petty court about a petty tyrant, Theocritus had come back to the sea and the sky and the
hardy pastoral life with a joy which touches some
of his lines with penetrating tenderness.   Better a

thousand times for him and for us the long, tranquil days under the pine and the olive than a great position under Hiero's hand and the weary intrigue and activity which made the melancholy semblance of a successful life for men less wise and genuine. The lines which the hand of Theocritus has left on the past are few and marvelously delicate, but they seem to gain distinctness from the remorseless years that have almost obliterated the features of the age in which he lived. It is better to see clearly one or two things in life than to move confused and blinded in the dust of an impotent activity ; it is better to hear one or two notes sung in the overshadowing trees than to spend one's years amid a murmur in which nothing is distinctly audible. Theocritus, shunning courts and cities, sought to assuage the pain of life at the heart of Nature, and did not seek in vain. He gave himself calmly and sincerely to the sweet and natural life which surrounded him, and in his tranquil self-surrender he gained, unsuspecting, the immortality denied his eager and restless cotemporaries. Life is so vast, so unspeakably rich, that to have reported accurately one swift glimpse, or to have preserved the melody of one rarely heard note, is to have mastered a part of the secret of the immortals.

Struggle and anguish have their place in every genuine life, but they are the stages through which it advances to a strength which is full of repose. The bursting of the calyx announces the flower ;

but the beauty of the perfect blossoming obliterated the very memory of its earlier growth. The climb upward is often a long anguish, but the dust and weariness are forgotten when once the eye rests on the vast outlook. "On every height there lies repose" is the sublime declaration of one who had looked into most things deeper than his fellows, and had learned much of the profounder processes of life. Emerson long ago noted that even in action the forms of the Greek heroes are always in repose ; the crudity of passion, the distorting agony of half-mastered purpose, are lost in a self-forgetfulness which borrows from Olympus something of the repose of the gods. The sublime calm which imparts to great works of art a hint of eternity is born of complete mastery of life ; all the stages of evolution have been accomplished, the whole movement of growth has been fulfilled, before the hand of art sets the seal of perfection on the thing that is done. Shadow and light, heat and cold, tempest and quiet days, have all wrought together before the blooming of the flower which in its perfect grace and beauty gives no hint of its troubled growth. As the consummation of all toil and struggle and anguish, there comes at last that deep repose, born not of idleness and indifference, but of the harmony of all the elements in their last and finest form.

In the unbroken silence of the noontide such thoughts come unbidden and almost unnoticed to one who surrenders himself to the hour and the scene. Nature has her tempests, but her harvests are gathered amid the calm of days that often seem filled with the peace of heaven, and the mighty and irresistible movement of her life goes on in unbroken silence. The deepest thoughts are always tranquilizing, the greatest minds are always full of calm, the richest lives have always at heart an unshaken repose.

CHAPTER XVIII.

EVENTIDE.

WHEN the shadows lengthen and the landscape becomes indistinct, the common life of men seems to touch the life of Nature most closely and sympathetically. The work of the day is accomplished; the sense of things to be done loses its painful tension; the mind, freed from the cares which engrossed it, opens unconsciously to the sights and sounds of the quiet hour. The fields are given over to silence and the gathering darkness; the roads cease to be thoroughfares of toil; and over all things the peace of night settles like an unspoken benediction. To the most preoccupied there comes a consciousness that the world has changed, and that, while the old framework remains intact, a strange and transforming beauty has touched and spiritualized it. At eventide one feels the soul of Nature as at no other hour. Her labors have ceased, her birds are silent; she, too, rests, and in ceasing to do for us she gives us herself. One by one the silvery points of light break out of the darkness overhead, and the faithful stars look down on the little earth they have watched over these countless years. The very names they bear recall the vanished races who waited for their appearing and counted them friends. Now that the lamps are lighted and the work of the day is done is it strange that the venerable mother, whose lullabies have soothed so many generations into sleep, should herself appeal to us in some intimate and personal way ?

With the fading out of shore and sea and forest line something deeper and more spiritual rises in the soul as the mists rise on the lowlands and over the surface of the waters. We surrender ourselves to it silently, reverently, and a change no less subtle and penetrating is wrought in us. Our personal ambitions, the sharply defined aims of our working hours, the very limitations of our individuality, are gone ; we lose ourselves in the larger life of which we are part. After the fret of the day we surrender ourselves to universal life as the bather, worn and spent, gives himself to the sea. There is no loss of personal force, but for an hour the individual activity is blended with the universal movement and the peace and quiet of infinity calm and restore the soul. Meditation comes with eventide as naturally as action with the morning ; our soul opens to the soul of Nature, and we discover anew that we are one. In the noblest passage in Latin poetry Lucretius invokes the universal spirit of Nature, and identifies it with the creative force which impels the stars and summons the flowers to strew themselves in the path of the sun. There is nothing so refreshing, so reinvigorating, as fresh contact with the fountain whence all visible life flows, as a renewed sense of oneness with the mighty appearance of things in which we live. Now that all outlines are softened, all distinctive features are lost, Nature loses its materialism, and becomes to our thought the vast, silent, unbroken flow of force which the later science has substituted for an earlier and cruder conception. And this invisible stream leads us back, as our thoughts unconsciously follow it, to One whose thought it is and whose mind shares with our mind something of the unsearchable mystery of its purpose and nature.

Some one has said that a man is great rather by reason of his unconscious thought than by reason of his deliberate and self-directed thinking. Released from meditation on definite and special themes, the thought of a great man instinctively returns to the mystery of life. No poet creates a Hamlet unless he has brooded long and almost unconsciously on the deeper things that make up the inner life ; such a figure, forever externalizing the profounder and more obscure phases of being, is born of secret and habitual contact with the deepest experiences and the most fundamental problems. The mind of a Shakespeare must often, forsaking the busy world of actuality, meditate in the twilight which seems to release the soul of things seen, and, veiling the actual, reveal the realities of existence.

Revery becomes of the highest importance when it substitutes for definite thinking that deep and silent meditation in which alone the soul comes to know itself and pierces the wonderful movement of things about it to its source and principle. One of Amiel's magical phrases is that in which he describes revery as the Sunday of the soul. Toil over, care banished, the world forgotten, one communes with that which is eternal. In the long course of centuries the forests are as short-lived as the flowers ; all visible forms are but momentary expressions of the creative force. In the work of the greatest mind all spoken and written thoughts are but partial and passing utterances of a life of whose volume and movement they afford only half-comprehended hints. After a Shakespeare has written thirty immortal plays he must still feel that what was deepest in him is unuttered. There is that below all expression of life which remains forever unspoken and unspeakable ; it is ours, but we cannot share it with others ; we drop our plummets into its depths in vain. It is deeper than our thought, and it is only at rare moments, when we surrender ourselves to ourselves, that the sense of what it contains and means fills us with a sudden and overpowering consciousness of immortality. Out of this deeper life all great thoughts rise into consciousness, losing much by imprisonment in any form of speech, but still bringing with them indubitable evidence of their more than royal birth. From time to time, like the elder race of prophets, they enter into our speech and renew the fading sense of the divinity of life, and so, through individual souls, the deeper truths are retold from generation to generation.

As one meditates in this evening hour, the darkness has gathered over the world and folded it out of sight. The few faint stars have become a shining host, and the immeasurable heavens have substituted for the near and familiar beauty of the earth their own sublime and awful commingling of unsearchable darkness and unquenchable light. So in every human life the near and the familiar is overarched by infinity and eternity.

CHAPTER XIX.

THE TURN OF THE TIDE.

For days past there have been intangible hints of change in earth and air ; the birds are silent, and the universal strident note of insect life makes more musical to memory the melodies of the earlier season. The sense of overflowing vitality which pervaded all things a few days ago, when the tide was at the flood, has gone ; the tide has turned, and already one sees the receding movement of the ebb. Through all the vanished months of flower and song, one's thought has traveled fast upon the advancing march of summer, trying to keep pace with it as it pushed its fragrant conquest northward ; to-day there is a brief interval of pause before the same thought, following the sunshine, turns south again, and seeks the tropics. A little later the spell of an indescribable peace will rest upon the earth, but a peace that will be but a brief truce between elements soon to close in struggle again. To-day, however, one feels the repose of a finished work before the first mellow touch of decay has come. The full, rich foliage still shelters the paths upon which the leaves have not yet fallen; the meadows are green; the skies soft and benignant. The conquest of summer is still intact, but here and there one sees slight but unmistakable evidence that the garrison, under cover of night, is beginning its long retreat. In such a moment one feels a sudden sense of loneliness, as if a friend were secretly preparing to desert one to his foes.

In this pause of the season one finds the subtle beauty and completeness of the summer growing upon him more and more. While the work was going forward, there was such profound interest in the process that one watched the turn and direction of the chisel rather than the surface of the marble slowly answering, line by line, the overmastering thought ; but now that the months of toil are past, and all the implements of labor are cast aside, the finished work absorbs all thought and fills all imaginations. So vast is it, and on such a scale of magnitude, that one hardly saw before the delicacy and exquisite adjustment of parts, the marvelous art that framed the smallest leaf and touched the vagrant wild flower still blooming on the edges of the woodland. It is, after all, when the great festival days are over and the thronging crowds have gone, that the true worshiper finds the temple beautiful with the highest visions of worship, and in the silence of deserted aisles and shrines sees with new wonder the workmanship of the Deity. For all such this is the most solemn of all the recurring Sabbaths of the year ; the hush at noonday and at even is itself an unspoken prayer. The moment of completion in the history of any great work is always sacred. When the noise and dust of the working days are gone, the great illuminating thought shines out unobscured ; and in the perception of this universal element, which on the instant wins recognition from every mind, the personal element vanishes ; the mere skill of the workman is forgotten in the new revelation of soul which it has given the world. For the same reason Nature takes on in these few and peaceful days a spiritual aspect, and the most careless finds himself touched, perhaps saddened, he knows not how or why.

Now again is the old mystery and deep secret of life forced upon thought : " Except a grain of wheat fall into the earth and die, it abideth by itself alone ; but if it die, it beareth much fruit." When the tide was at the flood it was enough to breathe the air and listen to the magical music of advancing life ; but now, when the tide begins to recede and leave the vast shores bare and silent, one must think, whether he will or not. Nature, that was careless poet, flower-crowned and buoyant with the promise of eternal youth, turns teacher, and will not suffer us to escape the deeper truths, the more searching and awful lessons. As the physical falls away the spiritual comes into clear and compelling distinctness. Who that goes abroad in these quiet days, and feels the subtle change from the grosser to the ethereal which pervades the very air, can escape the threefold thought of Life, Death, and Immortality ?

The silence that has already fallen upon the jubilant voices of summer will extend and deepen day by day until even the thoughtless babbling of the brooks ceases and the hush becomes universal. The earth, that a little time ago was producing such an endless variety of forms of life and beauty, will give birth to a myriad thoughts, deep, spiritual, and far-reaching ; translating into the language of spirit the vast movement of the year, and completing its mysterious cycle with a vision of the sublime ends for which Nature stands, and to the consummation of which all things are borne forward. And when the time is ripe there will come a transformation like the descent of the heavens upon the earth, flooding the dying world with unspeakable splendors ; the sunset which closes the long summer day and leaves through the night of winter the fadeless promise of another dawn.

CHAPTER XX.

A MEMORY OF SUMMER.

IN the pine woods, or floating under overhanging branches on the silent and almost motionless river, I have had visions of my study fire during the summer months, and, now that I find myself once more within the cheerful circle of its glow, the time that has passed since it was lighted for the last time in the spring seems like a long, delightful dream. I recall those charming days, some of them full of silence and repose from dawn to sunset, some of them ripe with effort and adventure, with a keen delight in the feeling of possession which comes with them ; they were brief, they have gone, but they are mine forever. The beauty and freshness that touched them morning after morning as the dew touches the flower are henceforth a part of my life ; they have entered into my soul as their light and heat entered into the ripening fruits and grains. I have come back to my friendly fire richer and wiser for my absence from its cheer and warmth ; my life has been renewed at those ancient sources whence all our knowledge has come ; I have felt again the solitude and sanctity of those venerable shades where the voices of the oracles were once heard, and fleeting glimpses of shy divinities made a momentary splendor in the dusky depths.

Wordsworth's sonnets are always within reach of those who never get beyond the compelling voice of nature, and who are continually returning to her with a sense of loss and decline after every wandering. As I take up the little, well-worn book, it opens of itself at a familiar page, and I read once more that sonnet which comes to one at times with an unspeakable pathos in its lines—a sense of permanent alienation and loss:

> " The world is too much with us ; late and soon,
> Getting and spending, we lay waste our powers ;
> Little we see in Nature that is ours ;
> We have given our hearts away, a sorbid boon.
> This sea that bares her bosom to the moon,
> The winds that will be howling at all hours,
> And are up-gathered now like springing flowers—
> For this, for everything, we are out of tune.
> It moves us not.   Great God ! I'd rather be
> A pagan suckled in a creed outworn,
> So might I, standing on this pleasant lea,
> Have glimpses that would make me less forlorn ;
> Have sight of Proteus rising from the sea,
> Or hear old Triton blow his wreathed horn."

Almost unconsciously I repeat these lines aloud, and straightway the fire, breaking into flame where it has been only glowing before, answers them with a sudden outburst of heat and light that make

a brief summer in my study.   When one goes back
to the woods and streams after long separation and
absorption in books and affairs, he misses something which once thrilled and inspired him.   The
meadows are unchanged, but the light that touched
them illusively, but with a lasting and incommunicable beauty, is gone ; the woodlands are dim and
shadowy as of old, but they are vacant of the presence that once filled them.   There is something
painfully disheartening in coming back to Nature
and finding one's self thus unwelcomed and uncared
for, and in the first moment of disappointment an
unspoken accusation of change and coldness lies
in the heart.   The change is not in Nature, however ; it is in ourselves.   "The world is too much
with us."   Not until its strife and tumult fade into
distance and memory will those finer senses, dulled
by contact with a meaner life, restore that which
we have lost.   After a little some such thought as
this comes to us, and day after day we haunt the
silent streams and the secret places of the forest ;
waiting, watching, unconsciously bringing ourselves
once more into harmony with the great, rich world
around us, we forget the tumult out of which we
have come, a deep peace possesses us, and in its
unbroken quietness the old sights and sounds
return again.   Youth, faith, hope, and love spring
again out of a soil which had begun to deny them
sustenance ; old dreams mingle with our waking
hours ; the old-time channels of joy, long silent

and bare, overflow with streams that restore a lost world of beauty in our souls. We have come back to Nature, and she has not denied us, in spite of our disloyalty.

I know of nothing more full of deep delight than this return of the old companionship, this restoration of the old intimacy. How much there is to recall, how many confidences there are to be exchanged ! The days are not long enough for all we would say and hear. Such hours come in the pine woods ; hours so full of the strange silence of the place, so unbroken by customary habits and thoughts, that no dial could divide into fragments a day that was one long unbroken spell of wonder and delight. So remote seemed all human life that even memory turned from it and lost herself in silent meditation ; so vast and mysterious was the life of Nature that the past and the future seemed part of the changeless present. The light fell soft and dim through the thickly woven branches and among the densely clustered trunks ; underneath, the deep masses of pine needles and the rich moss spread a carpet on which the heaviest footfall left the silence unbroken. It was a place of dreams and mysteries.

> " Heed the old oracles,
>   Ponder my spells ;
> Song wakes in my pinnacles
>   When the wind swells.
> Soundeth the prophetic wind,
> The shadows shake on the rock behind,

And the countless leaves of the pine are strings
Tuned to the lay the wood-god sings.
Hearken ! hearken !
If thou wouldst know the mystic song
Chanted when the sphere was young,
Aloft, abroad, the pæan swells ;
O wise man ! hear'st thou half it tells ?"

Sitting there, with the deep peace of the place sinking into the soul, the solitude was full of companionship ; the very silence seemed to give Nature a tone more commanding, an accent more thrilling. At intervals the gusts of wind reaching the borders of the wood filled the air with distant murmurs which widened, deepened, approached, until they broke into a great wave of sound overhead, and then, receding, died in fainter and ever fainter sounds. There was something in this sudden and unfamiliar roar of the pines that hinted at its kinship with the roar of the sea ; but it had a different tone. Waste and trackless solitudes and death are in the roar of the sea ; remoteness, untroubled centuries of silence, the strange alien memories of woodland life, are in the roar of the pines. The forgotten ages of an immemorial past seem to have become audible in it, and to speak of things which had ceased to exist before human speech was born ; things which lie at the roots of instinct rather than within the recollection of thought. The pines only murmur, but the secret which they guard so well is mine as well as theirs ; I am no alien in this secluded world ; my citizenship is here no less than in that other world to which I shall return, but to which I shall never wholly belong. The most solitary moods of Nature are not incommunicable; they may be shared by those who can forget themselves and hold their minds open to the elusive but potent influences of the forest. He who can escape the prison of habit and work and routine can say with Emerson :

> " When I am stretched beneath the pines,
> When the evening star so holy shines,
> I laugh at the lore and the pride of man,
> At the sophist schools and the learned clan ;
> For what are they all, in their high conceit,
> When man in the bush with God may meet ? "

IN THE FOREST OF ARDEN

Go with me : if you like, upon report,
The soil, the profit, and this kind of life,
I will your very faithful factor be,
And buy it with your gold right suddenly.

"AND I FOR ROSALIND."

CHAPTER XXI.

IN THE FOREST OF ARDEN.

I.

Under the greenwood tree,
Who loves to lie with me,
And turn his merry note
Unto the sweet bird's throat,
Come hither, come hither, come hither.

ROSALIND had just laid a spray of apple blossoms on the study table.

" Well," I said, " when shall we start ? "

" To-morrow."

Rosalind has a habit of swift decision when she has settled a question in her own mind, and I was not surprised when she replied with a single decisive word. But she also has a habit of making thorough preparation for any undertaking, and now she was quietly proposing to go off for the summer the very next day, and not a trunk was packed, not a seat secured in any train, not a movement made toward any winding up of household affairs. I had great faith in her ability to execute her plans with celerity, but I doubted whether she could be ready to turn the key in the door, bid farewell to the milkman and the butcher, and start the very next day for the Forest of Arden. For several past

seasons we had planned this bold excursion into
a country which few persons have seemed to know
much about since the day when a poet of great
fame, familiar with many strange climes and
peoples, found his way thither and shared the
golden fortune of his journey with all the world.
Winter after winter before the study fire, we had
made merry plans for this trip into the magical
forest ; we had discussed the best methods of traveling where no roads led ; we had enjoyed in anticipation the surmises of our neighbors concerning
our unexplained absence, and the delightful mystery
which would always linger about us when we had
returned, with memories of a landscape which no
eyes but ours had seen these many years, and of
rare and original people whose voices had been
silent in common speech so many generations that
only a few dreamers like ourselves even remembered that they had ever spoken. We had looked
along the library shelves for the books we should
take with us, until we remembered that in that
country there were books in the running streams.
Rosalind had gone so far as to lay aside a certain
volume of sermons whose aspiring note had more
than once made music of the momentary discords
of her life ; but I reminded her that such a work
would be strangely out of place in a forest where
there were sermons in stones. Finally we had de-
cided to leave books behind and go free-minded as
well as free-hearted. It had been a serious ques-

tion how much and what apparel we should take
with us, and that point was still unsettled when
the apple trees came to their blossoming. It is a
theory of mine that the chief delight of a vacation
from one's usual occupations is freedom from the
tyranny of plans and dates, and thus much Rosalind
had conceded to me.

There had been an irresistible charm in the very
secrecy which protected our adventure from the
curious and unsympathetic comment of the world.
We found endless pleasure in imagining what this
and that good neighbor of ours would say about
the folly of leaving a comfortable house, good
beds, and a well-stocked larder for the hard fare and
uncertain shelter of a strange forest. " For my
part," we gleefully heard Mrs. Grundy declare,—
" for my part, I cannot understand why two people
old enough to know better should make tramps of
themselves and go rambling about a piece of woods
that nobody ever heard of in the heat of the midsummer." Poor Mrs. Grundy! We could well
afford to laugh merrily at her scornful expostula-
tions; for while she was repeating platitudes to
overdressed and uninteresting people at Oldport,
we should be making sunny play of life with men
and women whose thoughts were free as the wind,
and whose hearts were fresh as the dew and the
stars. And often when our talk had died into
silence, and the wind without whistled to the fire
within, we had fallen to dreaming of those shadowy

aisles arched by the mighty trees, and of the splendid pageant that should make life seem as great and rich as Nature herself. I confess that all my dreams came to one ending ; that I should suddenly awake in some golden hour and really know Rosalind. Of course I had been coming through all these years to know something about Rosalind ; but in this busy world, with work to be done, and bills to be paid, and people to be seen, and journeys to be made, and friction and worry and fatigue to be borne, how can we really come to know one another ? We may meet the vicissitudes and changes side by side ; we may work together in the long days of toil ; our hearts may repose on a common trust, our thoughts travel a common road ; but how rarely do we come to the hour when the pressure of toil is removed, the clouds of anxiety melt into blue sky, and in the whole world nothing remains but the sun on the flower, and the song in the trees, and the unclouded light of love in the eyes ?

I dreamed, too, that in finding Rosalind I should also find myself. There were times when I had seemed on the very point of making this discovery, but something had always turned me aside when the quest was most eager and promising ; the world pressed into the seclusion for which I had struggled, and when I waited to hear its faintest murmur die in the distance, suddenly the tumult had risen again, and the dream of self-communion

and self-knowledge had vanished. To get out of
the uproar and confusion of things, I had often
fancied, would be like exchanging the dusty midsummer road for the shade of the woods where the
brook calms the day with its pellucid note of effort- ·
less flow, and the hours hide themselves from the
glances of the sun. In the forest of Arden I felt
sure I should find the repose, the quietude, the
freedom of thought, which would permit me to
know myself. There, too, I suspected Nature had
certain surprises for me ; certain secrets which she
has been holding back for the fortunate hour when
her spell would be supreme and unbroken. I even
hoped that I might come unaware upon that
ancient and perennial movement of life upon which
I seemed always to happen the very second after it
had been suspended ; that I might hear the note of
the hermit thrush breaking out of the heart of the
forest ; the soulful melody of the nightingale,
pathetic with unappeasable sorrow. In the Forest
of Arden, too, there were unspoiled men and
women, as indifferent to the fashion of the world
and the folly of the hour as the stars to the impalpable mist of the clouds ; men and women who
spoke the truth, and saw the fact, and lived the
right ; to whom love and faith and high hopes were
more real than the crowns of which they had been
despoiled and the kingdoms from which they had
been rejected. All this I had dreamed, and I
know not how many other brave and beautiful

dreams, and I was dreaming them again when Rosalind laid the apple blossoms on the study table, and answered, decisively, "To-morrow."

"To-morrow," I repeated ; "to-morrow. But how are you going to get ready ? If you sit up all night you cannot get through with the packing. You said only yesterday that your summer dress-making was shamefully behind. My dear, next week is the earliest possible time for our going."

Rosalind laughed archly, and pushed the apple blossoms over the woefully interlined manuscript of my new article on Egypt. There was in her very attitude a hint of unsuspected buoyancy and strength ; there was in her eyes a light which I have never seen under our uncertain skies. The breath of the apple blossoms filled the room, and a bobolink, poised on a branch outside the window, suddenly poured a rapturous song into the silence of the sweet spring day. I laid down my pen, pushed my scattered sheets into the portfolio, covered the inkstand, and laid my hand in hers. "Not to-morrow," I said, "not to-morrow. Let us go now."

II.

Now go we in content
To liberty and not to banishment.

I HAVE sometimes entertained myself by trying to imagine the impressions which our modern life would make upon some sensitive mind of a remote age. I have fancied myself rambling about New York with Montaigne, and taking note of his shrewd, satirical comment. I can hardly imagine him expressing any feeling of surprise, much less any sentiment of admiration ; but I am confident that under a masque of ironical self-complacency the old Gascon would find it difficult to repress his astonishment, and still more difficult to adjust his mind to evident and impressive changes. I have ventured at times to imagine myself in the company of another more remote and finely organized spirit of the past, and pictured to myself the keen, dispassionate criticism of Pericles on the things of modern habit and creation ; I have listened to his luminous interpretations of the changed conditions which he saw about him ; I have noted his unconcern toward the merely material advances of society, his penetrative insight into its intellectual and moral developments. A mind so capacious and open, a nature so trained and poised, could not be otherwise than self-contained and calm even in the presence of changes so vast and manifold as those which have transformed society since the days of the great Athenian ; but even he could not be quite unmoved if brought face to face with a life so unlike that with which he had been familiar ; there must come, even to one who feels the mastery of the soul over all conditions, a certain sense of wonder and awe.

It was with some such feeling that Rosalind and I found ourselves in the Forest of Arden. The journey was so soon accomplished that we had no time to accustom ourselves to the changes between the country we had left and that to which we had come. We had always fancied that the road would be long and hard, and that we should arrive worn and spent with the fatigues of travel. We were astonished and delighted when we suddenly discovered that we were within the boundaries of the Forest long before we had begun to think of the end of our journey. We had said nothing to each other by the way ; our thoughts were so busy that we had no time for speech. There were no other travelers ; everybody seemed to be going in the opposite direction ; and we were left to undisturbed meditation. The route to the Forest is one of those open secrets which whosoever would know must learn for himself ; it is impossible to direct those who do not discover for themselves how to make the journey. The Forest is probably the most accessible place on the face of the earth, but it is so rarely visited that one may go half a lifetime without meeting a person who has been there. I have never been able to explain the fact that those who have spent some time in the Forest, as well as those who are later to see it, seem to recognize each other by instinct. Rosalind and I happen to have a large circle of acquaintances, and it has been our good fortune to meet and recognize many who

were familiar with the Forest and who were able to
tell us much about its localities and charms.   It is
not generally known, and it is probably wise not to
emphasize the fact, that the fortunate few who have
access to the Forest form a kind of secret fraternity ; a brotherhood of the soul which is secret because those alone who are qualified for member-
ship by nature can understand either its language
or its aims.   It is a very strange thing that the
dwellers in the Forest never make the least attempt
at concealment, but that, no matter how frank and
explicit their statements may be, nobody outside
the brotherhood ever understands where the Forest
lies or what one finds when he gets there.   One
may write what he chooses about life in the Forest,
and only those whom Nature has selected and
trained will understand what he discloses ; to all
others it will be an idle tale or a fairy story for the
entertainment of people who have no serious busi-
ness in hand.

I remember well the first time I ever understood
that there is a Forest of Arden, and that they who
choose may wander through its arched aisles of
shade and live at their will in its deep and beautiful solitude ; a solitude in which nature sits like a
friend from whose face the veil has been with-
drawn, and whose strange and foreign utterance
has been exchanged for the most familiar speech.
Since that memorable afternoon under the apple
trees I have never been far from the Forest, al-

though at times I have lost sight of the line which its foliage makes against the horizon. I have always intended to cross that line some day and to explore the Forest ; perhaps even to make a home for myself there. But one's dreams must often wait for their realization, and so it has come to pass that I have gone all these years without personal familiarity with these beautiful scenes. I have since learned that one never comes to the Forest until he is thoroughly prepared in heart and mind, and I understand now that I could not have come earlier even if I had made the attempt. As it happened, I concerned myself with other things, and never approached very near the Forest, although never very far from it. I was never quite happy unless I caught frequent glimpses of its distant boughs, and I searched more and more eagerly for those who had left some record of their journeys to the Forest, and of their life within its magical boundaries. I discovered, to my great joy, that the libraries were full of books which had much to say about the delights of Arden : its enchanting scenery ; the music of its brooks ; the sweet and refreshing repose of its recesses ; the noble company that frequent it. I soon found that all the greater poets have been there, and that their lines had caught the magical radiance of the sky ; and many of the prose writers showed the same familiarity with a country in which they evidently found whatever was sweetest and best in life. I

came to know at last those whose knowledge of
Arden was most complete, and I put them in a
place by themselves ; a corner in the study to
which Rosalind and I went for the books we read
together. I would gladly give a list of these works
but for the fact I have already hinted—that those
who would understand their references to Arden
will come to know them without aid from me, and
that those who would not understand could find
nothing in them even if I should give page and
paragraph. It was a great surprise to me, when I
first began to speak of the Forest, to find that most
people scouted the very idea of such a country ;
many did not even understand what I meant.
Many a time, at sunset, when the light has lain soft
and tender on the distant Forest, I have pointed it
out, only to be told that what I thought was the
Forest was a splendid pile of clouds, a shining mass
of mist. I came to understand at last that Arden
exists only for a few, and I ceased to talk about it
save to those who shared my faith. Gradually I
came to number among my friends many who were
in the habit of making frequent journeys to the
Forest, and not a few who had spent the greater
part of their lives there. I remember the first time
I saw Rosalind I saw the light of the Arden sky in
her eyes, the buoyancy of the Arden air in her
step, the purity and freedom of the Arden life in
her nature. We built our home within sight of the
Forest, and there was never a day that we did not

talk about and plan our long-delayed journey thither.

"After all," said Rosalind, on that first glorious morning in Arden, "as I look back I see that we were always on the way here."

III.

Well, this is the Forest of Arden.

THE first sensation that comes to one who finds himself at last within the boundaries of the Forest of Arden is a delicious sense of freedom. I am not sure that there is not a certain sympathy with outlawry in that first exhilarating consciousness of having gotten out of the conventional world—the world whose chief purpose is that all men shall wear the same coat, eat the same dinner, repeat the same polite commonplaces, and be forgotten at last under the same epitaph. Forests have been the natural refuge of outlaws from the earliest time, and among the most respectable persons there has always been an ill-concealed liking for Robin Hood and the whole fraternity of the men of the bow. Truth is above all things characteristic of the dwellers in Arden, and it must be frankly confessed at the beginning, therefore, that the Forest is given over entirely to outlaws; those who have committed some grave offense against the world of conventions, or who have voluntarily gone into exile out of sheer liking for a freer life. These persons are not vulgar law-breakers ; they have neither blood on their hands nor ill-gotten gains in their pockets ; they are, on the contrary, people of uncommonly honest bearing and frank speech. Their offenses evidently impose small burden on their conscience, and they have the air of those who have never known what it is to have the Furies on one's track. Rosalind was struck with the charming naturalness and gayety of every one we met in our first ramble on that delicious and never-to-be-forgotten morning when we arrived in Arden. There was neither assumption or diffidence ; there was rather an entire absence of any kind of self-consciousness. Rosalind had fancied that we might be quite alone for a time, and we had expected to have a few days to ourselves. We had even planned in our romantic moments—and there is always a good deal of romance among the dwellers in Arden—a continuation of our wedding journey during the first week.

" It will be so much more delightful than before," suggested Rosalind, " because nobody will stare at us, and we shall have the whole world to ourselves." In that last phrase I recognized the ideal wedding journey, and was not at all dismayed at the prospect of having no society but Rosalind's for a time. But all such anticipations were dispelled in an hour. It was not that we met many people—it is one of the delights of the Forest that one finds society enough to take away the sense of isolation, but not enough to destroy the sweetness of solitude ; it was rather that the few we met made us feel at once that we had equal claim with them-selves on the hospitality of the place.   The Forest was not only free to every comer, but it evidently gave peculiar pleasure to those who were living in it to convey a sense of ownership to those who were arriving for the first time.   Rosalind declared that she felt as much at home as if she had been born there; and she added that she was glad she had brought only the dress she wore.   I was a little puzzled by the last remark ; it seemed not entirely logical. But I saw presently that she was expressing the fellowship of the place which forbade that one should possess anything that was not in use, and that, therefore, was not adding constantly to the common stock of pleasure.   Concerning the feel-ing of having been born in Arden, I became con-vinced later that there was good reason for believ-ing that everybody who loved the place had been born there, and that this fact explained the home feeling which came to one the instant he set foot within the Forest.   It is, in fact, the only place I have known which seemed to belong to me and to everybody else at the same time ; in which I felt no alien influence.   In our own home I had some-thing of the same feeling, but when I looked from a window or set foot from a door I was instantly oppressed with a sense of foreign ownership.   In

the great world how little could I call my own!
Only a few feet of soil out of the measureless landscape ; only a few trees and flowers out of all that
boundless foliage! I seemed driven out of the
heritage to which I was born ; cheated out of my
birthright in the beauty of the field and the mystery of the Forest ; put off with the beggarly por-
tion of a younger son when I ought to have fallen
heir to the kingdom. My chief joy was that from
the little space I called my own I could see the
whole heavens ; no man could rob me of that
splendid vision.

In Arden, however, the question of ownership
never comes into one's thoughts ; that the Forest
belongs to you gives you a deep joy, but there is a
deeper joy in the consciousness that it belongs to
everybody else.

The sense of freedom, which comes as strongly
to one in Arden as the smell of the sea to one who
has made a long journey from the inland, hints, I
suppose, at the offense which makes the dwellers
within its boundaries outlaws. For one reason or
another, they have all revolted against the rule of
the world, and the world has cast them out. They
have offended smug respectability, with its passion-
less devotion to deportment ; they have outraged
conventional usage, that carefully devised system
by which small natures attempt to bring great ones
down to their own dimensions ; they have scandal-
ized the orthodoxy which, like Memnon, has lost

the music of its morning, and marvels that the world no longer listens ; they have derided venerable prejudices—those ugly relics by which some men keep in remembrance their barbarous ancestry ; they have refused to follow flags whose battle were won or lost ages ago ; they have scorned to compromise with untruth, to go with the crowd, to acquiesce in evil " for the good of the cause," to speak when they ought to keep silent and to keep silent when they ought to speak. Truly the lists of sins charged to the account of Arden is a long one, and were it not that the memory of the world, concerned chiefly with the things that make for its comfort, is a short one, it would go ill with the lovers of the Forest. More than once it has happened that some offender has suffered so long a banishment that he has taken permanent refuge in Arden, and proved his citizenship there by some act worthy of its glorious privileges. In the Forest one comes constantly upon traces of those who, like Dante and Milton, have found there a refuge from the Philistinism of a world that often hates its children in exact proportion to their ability to give it light. For the most part, however, the outlaws who frequent the Forest suffer no longer banishment than that which they impose on themselves. They come and go at their own sweet will ; and their coming, I suspect, is generally a matter of their own choosing. The world still loves darkness more than light ; but it rarely nowadays falls upon the lantern-bearer and beats the life out of him, as in " the good old times." The world has grown more decent and polite, although still at heart no doubt the bad old world which stoned the prophets. It sneers where it once stoned ; it rejects and scorns where it once beat and burned. And so Arden has become a refuge, not so much from persecution and hatred as from ignorance, indifference, and the small wounds of small minds bent upon stinging that which they cannot destroy.

IV.

. . . . Fleet the time carelessly, as they did in the golden world.

Rosalind and I have always been planning to do a great many pleasant things when we had more time. During the busy days when we barely found opportunity to speak to each other we were always thinking of the better days when we should be able to sit hours together with no knock at the door and no imperative summons from the kitchen. Some man of sufficient eminence to give his words currency ought to define life as a series of interruptions. There are a good many valuable and inspiring things which can only be done when one is in the mood, and to secure a mood is not always an easy matter ; there are moods which are as coy as the most high-spirited woman, and must be wooed with as much patience and tact : and when the illusive prize is gained, one holds it by the frailest tenure. An interruption diverts the current, cuts the golden thread, breaks the exquisite harmony. I have often thought that Dante was far less unfortunate than the world has judged him to be. If he had been courted and crowned instead of rejected and exiled, it might have been that his genius would have missed the conditions which gave it immortal utterance. Left to himself, he had only his own nature to reckon with ; the world passed him by, and left him to the companionship of his sublime and awful dreams. To be left alone with one's self is often the highest good fortune. Moreover, I detest being hurried : it seems to me the most offensive way in which we are reminded of our mortality ; there is time enough if we know how to use it. People who, like Goethe, never rest and never haste, complete their work and escape the friction of it.

One of the most delightful things about life in Arden is the absence of any sense of haste ; life is a matter of being rather than of doing, and one shares the tranquillity of the great trees that silently expand year by year. The fever and restlessness are gone, the long strain of nerve and will relaxed ; a delicious feeling of having strength and time enough to live one's life and do one's work fills one with a deep and enduring sense of repose.

Rosalind, who had been busy about so many things that I sometimes almost lost sight of her for

days together, found time to take long walks with
me, to watch the birds and the clouds, and talk by
the hour about all manner of pleasant trifles. I
came to feel after a time that just what I anticipated would happen in Arden had happened. I
was fast becoming acquainted with her. We spent
days together in the most delightful half-vocal and
half-silent fellowship; leaving everything to the
mood of the hour and the place. Our walks took
us sometimes into lovely recesses, where mutual
confidences seemed as natural as the air ; sometimes into solitudes where talk seemed an impertinence, and we were silent under the spell of
rustling leaves and thrilling melodies coming from
we knew not what hidden minstrelsy. But whether
silent or speaking, we were fast coming to know
each other. I saw many traits in her, many characteristic habits and movements which I had never
noted before ; and I was conscious that she was
making similar discoveries in me. These mutual
revelations absorbed us during our first days in the
Forest ; and they confirmed the impression which
I brought with me that half the charm of people is
lost under the pressure of work and the irritation
of haste. We rarely know our best friends on their
best side ; our vision of their noblest selves is
constantly obscured by the mists of preoccupation
and weariness.

In Arden life is pitched on the natural key ; nobody is ever hurried ; nobody is ever interrupted ;

nobody carries his work like a pack on his back
instead of leaving it behind him as the sun leaves
the earth when the day is over and the calm stars
shine in the unbroken silence of the sky. Rosalind
and I were entirely conscious of the transformation
going on within us, and were not slow to submit
ourselves to its beneficent influence. We felt that
Arden would not put all its resources into our
hand until we had shaken off the dust and parted
from the fret of the world we had left behind.

In those first inspiring days we went oftenest to
the heart of the pines, where the moss grew so deep
that our movements were noiseless ; where the light
fell in subdued and gentle tones among the closely
clustered trees ; and where no sound ever reached
us save the organ music of the great boughs when
the wind evoked their sublime harmonies. Many
a time, as we have sat silent while the tones of that
majestic symphony rose and fell about us, we
seemed to become a part of the scene itself ; we
felt the unfathomed depth of a music produced by
no conscious thought, wrought out by no conscious
toil, but akin, in its spontaneity and naturalness,
with the fragrance of the flower. And with these
thrilling notes there came to us the thought of the
calm, reposeful, irresistible growth of Nature ;
never hasting, never at rest ; the silent spreading
of the tree, the steady burning of the star, the
noiseless flow of the river ! Was not this sublime
unconsciousness of time, this glorious appropria-

The heart of the Pines.

tion of eternity, something we had missed all our lives, and, in missing it, had lost our birthright of quiet hours, calm thought, sweet fellowship, ripening character ? The fever and tumult of the world we had left were discords in a strain that had never yielded its music before.

> For nature beats in perfect tune,
> And rounds with rhyme her every rune,
> Whether she work in land or sea,
> Or hide underground her alchemy.
> Thou canst not wave thy staff in air,
>   Or dip thy paddle in the lake,
> But it carves the bow of beauty there,
>   And the ripples in rhymes the oars forsake.

After one of these long, delicious days in the heart of the pines, Rosalind slipped her hand in mine as we walked slowly homeward.

"This is the first day of my life," she said.

V.

> And this our life, exempt from public haunt,
> Finds tongues in trees, books in the running brooks,
> Sermons in stones, and good in everything.

It was one of those entrancing mornings when the earth seems to have been made over under cover of night, and one drinks the first draft of a new experience when he sees it by the light of a new day. Such mornings are not uncommon in Arden, where the nightly dews work a perpetual miracle of freshness. On this particular morning we had strayed long and far, the silence and solitude of the woods luring us hour after hour with unspoken promises to the imagination. We had come at length to a place so secluded, so remote from stir and sound, that one might dream there of the sacredness of ancient oracles and the revels of ancient gods.

Rosalind had gathered wild flowers along the way, and sat at the base of a great tree intently disentangling her treasures. With that figure before me, I thought of nearer and more sacred things than the old woodland gods that might have strayed that way centuries ago ; I had no need to recall the vanished times and faiths to interpret the spirit of an hour so far from the commonplaces of human speech, so free from the passing moods of human life. The sweet unconsciousness of that face, bent over the mass of wild flowers, and akin to them in its unspoiled loveliness, was to that hour and place like the illuminated capital in the old missal ; a ray of color which unlocked the dark mystery of the text. When one can see the loveliness of a wild flower, and feel the absorbing charm of its sentiment, one is not far from the kingdom of Nature.

As these fancies chased one another across my mind, lying there at full length on the moss, I, too, seemed to lose all consciousness that I had ever touched life at any point than this, or that any other hour had ever pressed its cup of experience to my lips. The great world of which I was once part disappeared out of memory like 'a mist that recedes into a faint cloud and lies faint and far on the boundaries of the day; my own personal life, to which I had been bound by such a multitude of gossamer threads that when I tried to unloose one I seemed to weave a hundred in its place, seemed to sink below the surface of consciousness. I ceased to think, to feel ; I was conscious only of the vast and glorious world of tree and sky which surrounded me. I felt a thrill of wonder that I should be so placed. I had often lain thus under other trees, but never in such a mood as this. It was as if I had detached myself from the hitherto unbroken current of my personal life, and by some miracle of that marvelous place become part of the inarticulate life of Nature. Clouds and trees, dim vistas of shadow and flower-starred space of sunlight, were no longer alien to me ; I was akin with the vast and silent movement of things which encompassed me. No new sound came to me, no new sight broke on my vision ; but I heard with ears, and I saw with eyes, to which all other sounds and sights had ceased to be. I cannot translate into words the mystery and the thrill of that hour when, for the first time, I gave myself wholly into the keeping of Nature, and she received me as her child. What I felt, what I saw and heard, belong only to that place ; outside the Forest of Arden they are

incomprehensible. It is enough to say that I had
parted with all my limitations, and freed myself
from all my bonds of habit and ignorance and prej-
udice ; I was no longer worn and spent with work
and emotion and impression ; I was no longer
prisoned within the iron bars of my own personality. I was as free as the bird ; I was as little
bound to the past as the cloud that an hour ago
was breathed out of the heart of the sea ; I was as
joyous, as unconscious, as wholly given to the rapture of the hour as if I had come into a world
where freedom and joy were an inalienable and
universal possession. I did not speculate about
the great fleecy clouds that moved like galleons in
the ethereal sea above me ; I simply felt their
celestial beauty, the radiancy of their unchecked
movement, the freedom and splendor of the inexhaustible play of life of which they were part. I
asked no questions of myself about the great trees
that wove the garments of the magical forest about
me ; I felt the stir of their ancient life, rooted in
the centuries that had left no record in that place
save the added girth and the discarded leaf ; I had
no thought about the bird whose note thrilled the
forest save the rapture of pouring out without
measure or thought the joy that was in me ; I felt
the vast irresistible movement of life rolling, wave
after wave, out of the unseen seas beyond, obliter-
ating the faint divisions by which, in this working
world, we count the days of our toil, and making

all the ages one unbroken growth ; I felt the measureless calm, the sublime repose, of that uninter-
rupted expansion of form and beauty, from flower
to star and from bird to cloud ; I felt the mighty
impulse of that force which lights the sun in its
track and sets the stars to mark the boundaries of
its way.   Unbroken repose, unlimited growth, inexhaustible life, measureless force, unsearchable
beauty—who shall feel these things and not know
that there are no words for them !   And yet in
Arden they are part of every man's life !

And all the time Rosalind sat weaving her wild
flowers into a loose wreath.

" I must not take them from this place," she said,
as she bound them about the venerable tree, as one
would bind the fancy of the hour to some eternal
truth.

" Yesterday," she added, as she sat down again
and shook the stray leaves and petals from her
lap—" yesterday was the first day of my life : to-
day is the second."

It is one of the delights of Arden that one does
not need to put his whole thought into words there ;
half the need of language vanishes when we say
only what we mean, and what we say is heard with
sympathy and intelligence.   Rosalind and I were
thinking the same thought.   Yesterday we had
discovered that an open mind, freedom from work
and care and turmoil, make it possible for people
to be their true selves and to know each other.

To-day we had discovered that nature reveals herself only to the open mind and heart ; to all others she is deaf and dumb. The worldling who seeks her never sees so much as the hem of her garment ; the egotist, the self-engrossed man, searches in vain for her counsel and consolation ; the over-anxious, fretful soul finds her indifferent and incommunicable. We may seek her far and wide, with minds intent upon other things, and she will forever elude us ; but on the morning we open our windows with a free mind, she is there to break for us the seal of her treasures and to pour out the perfume of her flowers. She is cold, remote, inaccessible only so long as we close the doors of our hearts and minds to her. With the drudges and slaves of mere getting and saving she has nothing in common ; but with those who hold their souls above the price of the world and the bribe of success she loves to share her repose, her strength, and her beauty. In Arden Rosalind and I cared as little for the world we had left as children intent upon daisies care for the dust of the road out of which they have come into the wide meadows.

VI.

Here feel we but the penalty of Adam,
The season's difference, as the icy fang
And churlish chiding of the winter wind,
Which, when it bites and blows upon my body,
Even till I shrink with cold, I smile and say,
This is no flattery : these are counselors
That feelingly persuade me what I am.

IF the ideal conditions of life, of which most of us dream, could be realized, the result would be a padded and luxurious existence, well-housed, well-fed, well-dressed, with all the winds of heaven tempered to indolence and cowardice. We are saved from absolute shame by the consciousness that if such a life were possible we should speedily revolt against the comforts that flattered the body while they ignored the soul. In Arden there is no such compromise with our immoral desires to get results without work, to buy without paying for what we receive. Nature keeps no running accounts and suffers no man to get in her debt ; she deals with us on the principles of immutable righteousness ; she treats us as her equals, and demands from us an equivalent for every gift or grace of sight or sound she bestows. She rejects contemptuously the advances of the weaklings who aspire to become her beneficiaries without having made good their claim by some service or self-denial ; she rewards those only who, like herself, find music in the tempest as well as in the summer wind ; joy in arduous service as well as in careless ease. A world in which there were no labors to be accomplished, no burdens to be borne, no storms to be endured, would be a world without true joy, honest pleasure, or noble aspiration. It would be a fool's paradise.

The Forest of Arden is not without its changes of weather and season. Rosalind and I had fancied that it was always summer there, and that sunlight reigned from year's end to year's end ; if we had been told that storms sometimes overshadowed it, and that the icy fang of winter is felt there, we should have doubted the report. We had a good deal to learn when we first went to Arden ; in fact, we still have a great deal to learn about this wonderful country, in which so many of the ideals and standards with which we were once familiar are reversed. It is one of the blessed results of living in the Forest that one is more and more conscious that he does not know and more and more eager to learn. There are no shams of any sort in Arden, and all pride in concealing one's ignorance disappears ; one's chief concern is to be known precisely as he is. We were a little sensitive at first, a little disposed to be cautious about asking questions that might reveal our ignorance ; but we speedily lost the false shame we had brought with us from a world where men study to conceal, as a means of protecting, the things that are most precious to them. When we learned that in the Forest nobody vulgarizes one's affairs by making them matter of common talk, that all the meannesses of slander and gossip and misinterpretation are unknown, and that charity, courtesy, and honor are the unfailing law of intercourse, we threw down our reserves and experienced the refreshing freedom and sympathy of full knowledge between man and man.

After a long succession of golden days we awoke one morning to the familiar sound of rain on the roof ; there was no mistake about it ; it was raining in Arden ! Rosalind was so incredulous that I could see she doubted if she were awake ; and when she had satisfied herself of that fact she began to ask herself whether we had been really in the Forest at all ; whether we had not been dreaming in a kind of double consciousness, and had now come to the awakening which should rob us of this golden memory. At last we recognized the fact that we were still in Arden, and that it was raining. It was a melancholy awakening, and we were silent and depressed at breakfast ; for the first time no birds sang, and no sunlight flickered through the leaves and brought the day smiling to our very door. The rain fell steadily, and when the wind swept through the trees a sound like a sob went up from the Forest. After breakfast, for lack of active occupation, we lighted a few sticks in the rough fireplace, and found ourselves gradually drawn into the circle of cheer in the little room. The great world of Nature was for a moment out of doors, and there seemed no incongruity in talking about our own experiences ; we recalled the days in the world we had left behind ; we remembered the faces of our neighbors ; we reminded each other of the incidents of our journey ; we retold, in antiphonal fashion, the story of our stay in the Forest ; we grew eloquent as we described, one after another, the noble persons we had met there ; our hearts kindled as we became conscious of the wonderful enrichment and enlargement of life that had come to us ; and as the varied splendors of the days and scenes of Arden returned in our memories, the spell of the Forest came upon us, and the mysterious cadence of the rain, falling from leaf to leaf, added another and deeper tone to the harmony of our Forest life. The gloom had gone ; we had all the delight of a new experience in our hearts.

"I am glad it rains," Rosalind said, as she gave the fire one of her vigorous stirrings ; " I am glad it rains : I don't think we should have realized how lovely it is here if we were not shut in from time to time. One is played upon by so many impressions that one must escape from them to understand how beautiful they are. And then I'm not sure that even dark days and rain have not something which sunshine and clear skies could not give us." As usual, Rosalind had spoken my

thought before I had made it quite clear to myself ; I began to feel the peculiar delight of our
comfort in the heart of that great forest when the
storm was abroad. The monotone of the rain became rythmic with some ancient, primeval melody,
which the woods sang before their solitude had
been invaded by the eager feet of men always
searching for something which they do not possess.
I felt the spell of that mighty life which includes
the tempest and the tumult of winds and waves
among the myriad voices with which it speaks its
marvelous secret. Half the meaning would go out
of Nature if no storms ever dimmed the light of
stars or vexed the calm of summer seas. It is the
infinite variety of Nature which fits response to
every need and mood, renews forever the freshness
of contact with her, and holds us by a power of
which we never weary because we never exhaust its
resources.

" After all, Rosalind," I said, " it was not the
storms and the cold which made our old life hard,
and gave Nature an unfriendly aspect ; it was the
things in our human experience which gave tempest and winter a meaning not their own. In a
world in which all hearts beat true, and all hands
were helpful, there would be no real hardship in
Nature. It is the loss, sorrow, weariness, and disappointment of life which give dark days their
gloom, and cold its icy edge, and work its bitter-
ness. The real sorrows of life are not of Nature's

making ; if faithlessness and treachery and every sort of baseness were taken out of human lives, we should find only a healthy and vigorous joy in such hardship as Nature imposes upon us.   Upon men of sound, sweet life, she lays only such burdens as strength delights to carry, because in so doing it increases itself."

"That is true," said Rosalind.   "The day is dark only when the mind is dark ; all weathers are pleasant when the heart is at rest.   There are rainy days in Arden, but no gloomy ones ; there are probably cold days, but none that chill the soul."

I do not know whether it was Rosalind's smile or the sudden breaking of the sun through the clouds that made the room brilliant ; probably it was both. Rosalind opened the lattice, and I saw that the rain had ceased.   The drops still hung on every leaf, but the clouds were breaking into great shining masses, and the blue of the sky was of unsearchable purity and depth.   The sun poured a flood of light into the heart of the Forest, and suddenly every tiny drop, that a moment ago might have seemed a symbol of sorrow, held the radiant sun on its little disk, and every sphere shone as if a universe of fairy creation had been suddenly breathed into being.   And the splendor touched Rosalind also.

VII.

. . . . Pray you, if you know,
Where in the purlieus of this forest stands
A sheep-cote fenc'd about with olive trees ?

 * * * * *

The rank of osiers by the murmuring stream
Left on your right hand, brings you to the place.
But at this hour the house doth keep itself.

YEARS ago, when we were planning to build a
certain modest little house, Rosalind and I found
endless delight in the pleasures of anticipation.
By day and by night our talk came back to the
home we were to make for ourselves. We discussed plan after plan and found none quite to our
mind ; we examined critically the houses we
visited ; we pored over books ; we laid the experience of our friends under contribution ; and
when at last we had agreed upon certain essentials
we called an architect to our aid, and fondly im-
agined that now the prelude of discussion and
delay was over, we should find unalloyed delight in
seeing our imaginary home swiftly take form and
become a thing of reality. Alas for our hopes !
Expense followed fast upon expense and delay
upon delay. There were endless troubles with
masons and carpenters and plumbers ; and when
our dream was at last realized, the charm of it had
somehow vanished ; so much anxiety, care, and
vexation had gone into the process of building that

the completed structure seemed to be a monument
of our toil rather than a refuge from the world.

After this sad experience, Rosalind and I con-
tented ourselves with building castles in Spain ;
and so great has been our devotion to this occupation that we are already joint owners of immense
possessions in that remote and beautiful country.
It is a singular circumstance that the dwellers in
Arden, almost without exception, are holders of
estates in Spain.   I have never seen any of these
splendid properties ; in fact, Rosalind and I have
never seen our own castles ; but I have heard very
full and graphic descriptions of those distant seats.
In imagination I have often seen the great piles
crowning the crests of wooded hills, whence noble
parks and vast landscapes lay spread out ; I have
been thrilled by the notes of the hunting-horn and
discerned from afar the cavalcade of beautiful
women and gallant men winding its way to the
gates of the courtyard ; I have seen splendid ban-
ners afloat from turret and casement ; I have seen
lights flashing at night and heard faint murmurs of
music and laughter.   Truly they are fortunate who
own castles in Spain !

In the Forest of Arden there is no such brave
show of battlement and rampart.   In all our
rambles we never came upon a castle or palace; in
fact, so far as I remember, no one ever spoke of
such structures.   They seem to have no place
there.   Nor is it hard to understand this singular

divergence from the ways of a world whose habits and standards are continually reversed in the Forest. In castle and palace, the wealth and splendor of life,—everything that gives it grace and beauty to the eye,—are treasured within massive walls and protected from the common gaze and touch. Every great park, with its reaches of inviting sward and its groups of noble trees, seems to say to those who pass along the highway : " We are too rare for your using." Every stately palace, with its wonderful paintings and hangings, its sculpture and furnishings, locks its massive gates against the great world without, as if that which it guards were too precious for common eyes. In Arden no one dreams of fencing off a lovely bit of open meadow or a cluster of great trees ; private ownership is unknown in the Forest. Those who dwell there are tenants in common of a grander estate than was ever conquered by sword, purchased by gold, or bequeathed by the laws of descent. There are homes for privacy, for the sanctities of love and friendship ; but the wealth of life is common to all. Instead of elegant houses, and a meager, inferior public life, as in the great cities of the world, there are modest homes and a noble common life. If the houses in our cities were simple and home-like in their appointments, and all their treasures of art and beauty were lodged in noble structures, open to every citizen, the world would know something of the habits of those who find in Arden that satisfying thought of life which is denied them among men. Moderation, simplicity, frugality for our private and personal wants ; splendid profusion, noble lavishness, beautiful luxury for that common life which now languishes because so few recognize its needs. When will the world learn the real lesson of civilization, and, for the cheap and ignoble aspect of modern cities, bring back the stateliness of Rome and the beauty of that wonderful city whose poetry and art were but the voices of her common life ?

The murmuring stream at our door in Arden whispered to us by day and by night the sweet secret of the happiness in the Forest, where no man strives to outshine his neighbor or to encumber the free and joyous play of his life with those luxuries which are only another name for care. Our modest little home sheltered but did not enslave us ; it held a door open for all the sweet ministries of affection, but it was barred against anxiety and care ; birds sang at its flower-embowered windows, and the fragrance of the beautiful days lingered there, but no sound from the world of those that strive and struggle ever entered. We were joyous as children in a home which protected our bodies while it set our spirits at liberty ; which gave us the sweetness of rest and seclusion, while it left us free to use the ample leisure of the Forest and to drink deep of its rich and healthful life. Vine-covered, overshadowed by the pine, with the olive standing in friendly neighborhood, our home in Arden seemed at the same time part of the Forest and part of ourselves. If it had grown out of the soil, it could not have fitted into the landscape with less suggestion of artifice and construction ; indeed, Nature had furnished all the materials, and when the simple structure was complete she claimed it again and made it her own with endless device of moss and vine. Without, it seemed part of the Forest ; within, it seemed the visible history of our life there. Friends came and went through the unlatched door ; morning broke radiant through the latticed window ; the seasons enfolded it with their changing life ; our own fellowship of mind and heart made it unspeakably sacred. Love and loyalty within ; noble friends at the hearthstone ; soft or shining heavens above ; mystery of forest and music of stream without : this is home in Arden.

VIII.

. . . . books in the running brooks.

In the days before we went to Arden, Rosalind and I had often wondered what books we should find there, and we had anticipated with the keenest curiosity that in the mere presence or absence of certain books we should discover at last the final principle of criticism, the absolute standard of literary art. Many a time as we sat before the study fire and finished the reading of some volume that had yielded us unmixed delight, we had said to each other that we should surely find it in Arden, and read it again in an atmosphere in which the most delicate and beautiful meanings would become as clear as the exquisite tracery of frost on the study windows. That we should find all the classics there we had not the least doubt ; who could imagine a community of intelligent persons without Homer and Dante and Shakespeare and Wordsworth ! How the volumes would be housed we did not try to divine ; but that we should find them there we did not think of doubting. Our chief thought was of the principle of selection, long sought after by lovers of books but never yet found, which we were certain would be easily discovered when we came to look along the shelves of the libraries in Arden. With what delight we anticipated the long days when we should read together again, and amid such novel surroundings, the books we loved ! For, although our home contained few luxuries, it had fed the mind ; there was not a great soul in literature whose name was not on the shelves of our library, and the companionships of that room made our quiet home more rich in gracious and noble influences than many a palace.

And yet we had been in the Forest several months before we even thought of books ; so absorbed were we in the noble life of the place, in the inspiring society about us. There came a morning, however, when, as I looked out into the shadows of the deep woods, I recalled a wonderful line of Dante's that must have come to the poet as he passed through some silent and somber woodland path. Suddenly I remembered that months had passed since we had opened a book; we whose most inspiring hours had once been those in which we read together from some familiar page. For an instant I felt something akin to remorse; it seemed as if I had been disloyal to friends who had never failed me in any time of need. But as I meditated on this strange forgetfulness of mine, I saw that in Arden books have no place and serve no purpose. Why should one read a translation when the original work lies open and legible before him? Why should one watch the reflections in the shadowy surface of the lake when the heavens shine above him? Why should one linger before the picturesque landscape which art has imperfectly transferred to canvas when the scene, with all its elusive play of light and shade, lies outspread before him? I became conscious that in Arden one lives habitually in the world which books are always striving to portray and interpret; that one sees with his own eyes all that the eyes of the keenest observer have ever seen; that one feels in his own soul all the greatest soul has ever felt. That which in the outer world most men know only by report, in Arden each one knows for himself. The stories of travelers cease to interest us when we are at last within the borders of the strange, far country.

Books are, at the best, faint and imperfect transcriptions of Nature and life ; when one comes to see Nature as she is with his own eyes, and to enter into the secrets of life, all transcriptions become inadequate. He who has heard the mysterious and haunting monotone of the sea will never rest content with the noblest harmony in which the composer seeks to blend those deep, elusive tones ; he who has sat hour by hour under the spell of the deep woods will feel that spell shorn of its magical power in the noblest verse that ever sought to contain and express it ; he who has once looked with clear, unflinching gaze into the depths of human life will find only vague shadows of the mighty realities in the greatest drama and fiction. The eternal struggle of art is to utter these unutterable things ; the immortal thirst of the soul will lead it again and again to these ancient fountains, whence it will bring back its handful of water in vessels curiously carven by the hands of imagination. But no cup of man's making will ever hold all that fountain has to give, and to those who are really athirst these golden and beautifully wrought vessels are insufficient ; they must drink of the living stream.

In Arden we found these ancient and perennial fountains; and we drank deep and long. There was that in the mystery of the woods which made all poetry seem pale and unreal to us; there was that in life, as we saw it in the noble souls about us, which made all records and transcriptions in books seem cold and superficial. What need had we of verse when the things which the greatest poets had seen with vision no clearer than ours lay clear and unspeakably beautiful before us? What had fiction or history for us, upon whom the thrilling spell of the deepest human living was laid! Rosalind and I were hourly meeting those whose thoughts had fed the world for generations, and whose names were on all lips, but they never spoke of the books they had written, the pictures they had painted, the music they had composed. And, strange to say, it was not because of these splendid works that we were drawn to them; it was the quality of their natures, the deep, compelling charm of their minds, which filled us with joy in their companionship. In Arden it is a small matter that Shakespeare has written "Hamlet," or Wordsworth the "Ode on Immortality"; not that which they have accomplished but that which they are in themselves gives these names a luster in Arden such as shines from no crown of fame in the outer world. Rosalind and I had dreamed that we might meet some of those whose words had been the food of immortal hope to us, but we almost dreaded that nearer acquaintance which might dispel the illusion of superiority. How delighted were we to discover that not only are great souls, really understood, greater than all their works, but that the works were forgotten and nothing was remembered but the soul! Not as those who are fed by the bounty of the king, but as kings ourselves, were we received into this noble company. Were we not born to the same inheritance? Were not Nature and life ours as truly as they were Shakespeare's and Wordsworth's? As we sat at rest under the great arms of the trees, or roamed at will through the woodland paths, the one thought that was common to us all was, not how nobly these scenes had been pictured and spoken, but how far above all language of art they were, and how shallow runs the stream of speech when these mysterious treasures of feeling and insight are launched upon it!

IX.

. . . . every day
Men of great worth resorted to this forest.

THE friendship of Nature is matched in Arden with human friendships, as sincere, as void of disguise and flattery, as stimulating and satisfying. There are times when every sensitive person is wounded by misunderstanding of motives, by lack of sympathy, by indifference and coldness; such

hours came not infrequently to Rosalind and myself in the old days before we set out for the Forest.
We found unfailing consolation and strength in our
common faith and purpose, but the frigidity of the
atmosphere made us conscious at times of the effort
one puts forth to simply sustain the life of his
ideals, the charm and sweetness of those secret
hopes which feed the soul. What must it be to live
among those who are quick to recognize nobility of
motive, to conspire with aspiration, to believe in
the best and highest in each other? It was to taste
such a life as this, to feel the consoling power of
mutual faith and the inspiration of a common devotion to the ideals that were dearest to us, that
our thoughts turned so often and with such longing to Arden. In such moments we opened with
delight certain books which were full of the joy
and beauty of the Forest life ; books which brought
back the dreams that were fading out and touched
us afresh with the unsearchable charm and beauty
of the Ideal. Surely there could no better fortune
befall us than to be able to call these great minis-
tering spirits our friends.

But, strong as was our longing, we were not
without misgivings when we first found ourselves
in Arden. In this commerce of ideas and hopes,
what had we to give in exchange? How could we
claim that equality with those we longed to know
which is the only basis of friendship? We were
unconsciously carrying into the Forest the limi-

tations of our old life, and among all the glad surprises that awaited us, there was none so joyful as
the discovery that our misgivings vanished as soon
as we began to know our neighbors. Neither of
us will ever forget the perfect joy of those earliest
meetings ; a joy so great that we wondered if it
could endure. There is nothing so satisfying as
quick comprehension of one's hopes, instant sympathy with them, absolute frankness of speech, and
the brilliant and stimulating play of mind upon
mind where there is complete unconsciousness of
self and complete absorption in the idea and the
hour. There was something almost intoxicating
in those first wonderful talks in Arden ; we seemed
suddenly not only to be perfectly understood by
others, but for the first time to understand ourselves ; the horizons of our mental world seemed
to be swiftly receding and new continents of truth
were lifted up into the clear light of consciousness.
All that was best in us was set free ; we were confident where we had been uncertain and doubtful ;
we were bold where we had been almost cowardly.
We spoke our deepest thought frankly ; we drew
from their hiding-places our noblest dreams of the
life we hoped to live and the things we hoped to
achieve ; we concealed nothing, reserved nothing,
evaded nothing ; we were desirous above all things
that others should know us as we knew ourselves.
It was especially restful and refreshing to speak of
our failures and weaknesses, of our struggles and

defeats ; for these experiences of ours were instantly matched by kindred experiences, and in the
common sympathy and comprehension a new kind
of strength came to us. The humiliation of defeat
was shared, we found, by even the greatest ; and
that which made these noble souls what they were
was not freedom from failure and weakness, but
steadfast struggle to overcome and achieve. As
the life of a new hope filled our hearts, we remembered with a sudden pain the world out of which
we had escaped, where every one hides his weakness lest it feed a vulgar curiosity, and conceals his
defeats lest they be used to destroy rather than to
build him up.

With what delight did we find that in Arden the
talk touched only great themes, in a spirit of beautiful candor and unaffected earnestness ! To have
exchanged the small personal talk from which we
had often been unable to escape for this simple,
sincere discourse on the things that were of
common interest was like exchanging the cloud-en-
veloped lowland for some sunny mountain slope,
where every breath was vital and one mused on half
a continent spread out at his feet. There is no
food for the soul but truth, and we were filled with
a mighty hunger when we understood for how long
a time we had been but half fed. A new strength
came to us, and with it an openness of mind and a
responsiveness of heart that made life an inexhaustible joy. We were set free from the weariness of

old struggles to make ourselves understood; we were no longer perplexed with doubts about the reality of our ideas; we had but to speak the thought that was in us, and to live fearlessly and joyously in the hour that was before us. Frank speaking, absolute candor, that would once have wounded, now only cheered and stimulated; the spirit of entire helpfulness drives out all morbid self-consciousness. Differences no longer embitter when courtesy and faith are universal possessions.

There is nothing more sacred than friendship, and it is impossible to profane it by drawing the veil from its ministries. The charm of a perfectly noble companionship between two souls is as real as the perfume of a flower, and as impossible to convey by word or speech; Nature has made its sanctity inviolable by making it forever impossible of revelation and transference. I cannot translate into any language the delicate charm, the inexhaustible variety, the noble fidelity to truth, the vigor and splendor of thought, the unfailing sympathy, of our Arden friendships; they are a part of the Forest, and one must seek them there. It would vulgarize these fellowships to catalogue the great names, always familiar to us, and yet which gained another and a better familiarity when they ceased to recall famous persons and became associated with those who sat at our hearthstone or gathered about our simple board. Rosalind was sooner at home in this noble company than I: she had far less to learn;

but at last I grew into a familiarity with my neighbors which was all the sweeter to me because it
registered a change in myself long hoped for, often
despaired of, at last accomplished. To be at one
with Nature was a joy which made life seem rich
beyond all earlier thought; but when to this there
was added the fellowship of spirits as true and
great as Nature herself, the wine of life overflowed
the exquisite cup into which an invisible hand
poured it. The days passed like a dream as we
strayed together through the woodland paths;
sometimes in some deep and shadowy glen silence
laid her finger on our lips, and in a common mood
we found ourselves drawn together without speech.
Often at night, when the magic of the moon has
woven all manner of enchantments about us, we
have lingered hour after hour under that supreme
spell which is felt only when soul speaks with soul.

X.

. . . . there's no clock in the forest.

THERE were a great many days in Arden when
we did absolutely nothing; we awoke without
plans; we fell asleep without memories. This was
especially true of the earlier part of our stay in the
Forest; the stage of intense enjoyment of new-
found freedom and repose. There was a kind of
rapture in the possession of our days that was new

to us ; a sense of ownership of time of which we
had never so much as dreamed when we lived by
the clock.   Those tiny ornamental hands on the
delicately painted dial were our taskmasters, dis-
guised under forms so dainty and fragile that, while
we felt their tyranny, we never so much as suspected their share in our servitude.   Silent themselves, they issued their commands in tones we
dared not disregard ; fashioned so cunningly, they
ruled us as with iron scepters ; moving within so
small a circle, they sent us hither and yon on every
imaginable service.   They severed eternity into
minute fragments, and dealt it out to us minute by
minute like a cordial given drop by drop to the
dying ; they marked with relentless exactness the
brief periods of our leisure and indicated the hours
of our toil.   We could not escape from their vigi-
lant and inexorable surveillance ; day and night
they kept silent record beside us, measuring out
the golden light of summer in their tiny balances,
and doling out the pittance of winter sunshine with
niggardly reluctance.   They hastened to the end of
our joys, and moved with funereal slowness through
the appointed times of our sorrow.   They ruled
every season, pervaded every day, recorded every
hour, and, like misers hoarding a treasure, doled
out our birthright of leisure second by second ; so
that, being rich, we were always impoverished ;
inheritors of vast fortune, we were put off with a
meager income ; born free, we were servants of

masters who neither ate nor slept, that they might never for a second surrender their overseership.

There are no clocks in Arden ; the sun bestows the day, and no impertinence of men destroys its charm by calculating its value and marking it with a price. The only computers of time are the great trees whose shadows register the unbroken march of light from east to west. Even the days and nights lost that painful distinctness which they had for us when they gave us a constant sense of loss, an incessant apprehension of change and age. Their shining procession leaves no such records in Arden ; they come like the waves whose ceaseless flow sings of the boundless sea whence they come. They bring no consciousness of ebbing years and joys and strength ; they bring rather a sense of eternal resource and beneficence. In Arden one never feels in haste ; there is always time enough and to spare ; in fact, the word time is never used in the vernacular of the Forest except when reference is made to the enslaved world without. There were moments at the beginning when we felt a little bewildered by our freedom, and I think Rosalind secretly longed for the familiar tones of the cuckoo clock which had chimed so many years in and out for us in the old days. One must get accustomed even to good fortune, and after one has been con-fined within the narrow limits of a little plot of earth the possession of a continent confuses and perplexes. But men are born to good fortune if they but knew it, and we were soon reconciled to the possession of inexhaustible wealth. We felt the delight of a sudden exchange of poverty for richness, a swift transition from bondage to freedom. Eternity was ours, and we ceased to divide it into fragments, or to set it off into duties and work. We lived in the consciousness of a vast leisure; a quiet happiness took the place of the old anxiety to always do at the moment the thing that ought to be done; we accepted the days as gifts of joy rather than as bringers of care.

It was delightful to fall asleep lulled by the rustle of the leaves, and to awake, without memory of care or pressure of work, to a day that had brought nothing more discordant into the Forest than the singing of birds. We rose exhilarated and buoyant, and breakfasted merrily under a great oak; sometimes we lingered far on into the morning, yielding ourselves to the spell of the early day when it no longer proses of work and duty, but sings of freedom and ease and the strength that makes a play of life. Often we strayed without plan or purpose, as the winding paths of the Forest led us; happy and care-free as children suddenly let loose in fairyland. We discovered moss-grown paths which led into the very heart of the Forest, and we pressed on silently from one green recess to another until all memory of the sunnier world faded out of mind. Sometimes we emerged suddenly into a wide, brilliant glade; sometimes we came into a sanctuary so overhung with great masses of foliage, so secluded and silent, that we took the rude pile of moss-grown stones we found there as an altar to solitude, and our stillness became part of the universal worship of silence which touched us with a deep and beautiful solemnity. Wherever we strayed the same tranquil leisure enfolded us ; day followed day in an order unbroken and peaceful as the unfolding of the flowers and the silent march of the stars. Time no longer ran like the few sands in a delicate hour-glass held by a fragile human hand, but like a majestic river fed by fathomless seas. The sky, bare and free from horizon to horizon, was itself a symbol of eternity, with its infinite depth of color, its sublime serenity, its deep silence broken only by the flight and songs of birds. These were at home in that ethereal sphere, at rest in that boundless space, and we were not slow to learn the lesson of their freedom and joy. We gave ourselves up to the sweetness of that unmeasured life, without thought of yesterday or to-morrow ; we drank the cup which to-day held to our lips, and knew that so long as we were athirst that draught would not be denied us.

XI.

> . . . . every of this happy number
> That have endur'd shrewd nights and days with us,
> Shall share the good of our returned fortune,
> According to the measure of their states.

THERE is this great consolation for those who cannot live continually in the Forest of Arden: that, having once proven one's citizenship there, one can return at will. Those who have lived in Arden and have gone back again into the world, are sustained in their loneliness by the knowledge of their fellowship with a nobler community. Aliens though they are, they have yet a country to which they are loyal, not through interest, but through aspiration, imagination, faith, and love. Rosalind and I found the months in Arden all too brief; our life there was one long golden day, whose sunset cast a soft and tender light on our whole past and made it beautiful for us. It is one of the delights of the Forest that only the noblest aspects of life are visible there; or, rather, that the hard and bare details of living, seen in the atmosphere of Arden, yield some truth of character or experience which, like the rose, makes even the rough calyx which encased it beautiful. We had sometimes spoken together of our return to the world we had left, but we put off as long as possible all definite preparations. I am not sure that I should ever have come back if Rosalind had not taken the matter into her own hands. She remembered that there was work to be done which ought not to be longer postponed ; that there were duties to be met which ought not to be longer evaded ; and when did Rosalind fail to be or to do that which the hour and the experience commanded? We treasured the last days as if the minutes were pure gold ; we lingered in talk with our friends as if we should never again hear such spoken words ; we loitered in the woods as if the spell of that beautiful silence would never again touch us. And yet we knew that, once possessed, these things were ours forever ; neither care, nor change, nor time, nor death, could take them from us, for henceforth they were part of ourselves.

We stood again at length on the little porch, covered with dust, and turned the key in the unused lock. I think we were both a little reluctant to enter and begin again the old round of life and work. The house seemed smaller and less homelike, the furniture had lost its freshness, the books on the shelves looked dull and faded. Rosalind ran to a window, opened it, and let in a flood of sunshine. I confess I was beginning to feel a little heartsick, but when the light fell on her I remembered the rainy day in Arden, when the first rays after the storm touched her and dispelled the gloom, and I realized, with a joy too deep for words or tears, that I had brought the best of Arden with me. We talked little during those first days of our home-coming, but we set the house in order, we recalled to the lonely rooms the old associations, and we quietly took up the cares and burdens we had dropped. It was not easy at first, and there were days when we were both heartsore ; but we waited and worked and hoped. Our neighbors found us more silent and absorbed than of old, but neither that change nor our absence seemed to have made any impression upon them. Indeed, we even doubted if they knew that we had taken such a journey. Day by day we stepped into the old places and fell into the old habits, until all the broken threads of our life were reunited and we were apparently as much a part of the world as if we had never gone out of it and found a nobler and happier sphere.

But there came to us gradually a clear consciousness that, though we were in the world, we were not of it, nor ever again could be. It was no longer our world ; its standards, its thoughts, its pleasures, were not for us. We were not lonely in it ; on the contrary, when the first impression of strangeness wore off, we were happier than we had ever been in the old days. Our reputation was no longer in the breath of men ; our fortune was no longer at the mercy of rising or falling markets ; our plans and hopes were no longer subject to chance and change. We had a possession in the Forest of Arden, and we had friends and dreams there beyond the empire of time and fate. And when we compared the security of our fortunes with the vicissitudes to

which the estates of our neighbors were exposed ;
when we compared our noble-hearted friends with
their meaner companionships ; when we compared
the peaceful serenity of our hearts with their perplexities and anxieties, we were filled with inexpress-
ible sympathy. We no longer pierced them with
the arrows of satire and wit because they accepted
lower standards and found pleasure in things essen-
tially pleasureless ; they had not lived in Arden,
and why should we berate them for not possessing
that which had never been within their reach ? We
saw that upon those whom an inscrutable fate has
led through the paths of Arden a great and noble
duty is laid. They are not to be the scorners and
despisers of those whose eyes are holden that they
cannot see, and whose ears are stopped that they
cannot hear, the vision and the melody of things
ideal. They are rather to be eyes to the blind and
ears to the deaf. They are to interpret in unshaken
trust and patience that which has been revealed to
them ; servants are they of the Ideal, and their
ministry is their exceeding great reward. So long
as they see clearly, it is small matter to them that
their message is rejected, the mighty consolation
which they bring refused ; their joy does not hang
on acceptance or rejection at the hands of their fellows. The only real losers are those who will not
see nor hear. It is not the light-bringer who suffers
when the torch is torn from his hands ; it is those
whose paths he would lighten.

And more and more, as the days went by, Rosalind and I found the life of the Forest stealing into our old home. The old monotony was gone; the old weariness and depression crossed our threshold no more. If work was pressing, we were always looking through and beyond it; we saw the fine results that were being accomplished in it ; we recognized the high necessity which imposed it. If perplexities and cares sat with us at the fireside, we received them as friends; for in the light of Arden had we not seen their harsh masks removed, and behind them the benignant faces of those who patiently serve and minister, and receive no reward save fear and avoidance and misconception? In fact, having lived in Arden, and with the consciousness that we might seek shelter there as in another and securer home, the world barely touched us, save to awaken our sympathies and to evoke our help. It had little to give us; we had much to give it. There was within and about us a peace and joy which were not for us alone. Our little home was folded within impalpable walls, and beyond it lay a vision of green foliage and golden masses of cloud that never faded off the horizon. There were benignant presences in our rooms visible to no eyes but ours ; for our Arden friends did not forsake us. There were memories between us which made all our days beautiful with the consciousness of immortal faith and love ; there were hopes which, like celestial beings, looked upon us with eyes deep with unspeakable prophecy as they waited at the doors of the future.

It is an autumn afternoon, and the sun lies warm on the ripening vines that cover the wall, and on the late flowers that bloom by the roadside. As I write these words I look up from my portfolio, and Rosalind sits there, work in hand, smiling at me over her flying needle. My glance rests on her a moment, and a strange uncertainty comes over me. Have I really been in Arden, or have I dreamed these things, looking into Rosalind's eyes ? It matters little whether I have traveled or dreamed ; where Rosalind is, there, for me at least, lies the Forest of Arden.

AN UNDISCOVERED ISLAND.

———

" Where should this music be ? i' the air, or th' earth ?
It sounds no more : and, sure, it waits upon
Some god o' the island."

CHAPTER XXII.

AN UNDISCOVERED ISLAND.

I.

Come unto these yellow sands,
And then take hands ;
Curtsied when you have, and kiss'd
The wild waves whist,
Foot it featly here and there ;
And, sweet sprites, the burden bear.

ONE winter evening, some time after the memorable year of our first visit to the Forest of Arden, Rosalind and I were planning a return to that enchanting place, and in the glow of the fire on the hearth were picturing to ourselves the delights that would be ours again, when the clang of the knocker suddenly recalled us from our dreams. Hospitably inclined, as I trust and believe we are, at that moment an interruption seemed like an intrusion. But our momentary annoyance was speedily dispelled when the library door opened, and, with the freedom which belongs to old friendship, the Poet entered unannounced. No one could have been more welcome on that wintry night than this genial and human soul, bound to us by many ties of

familiar association as well as by frequent neighbor-
liness in the woods of Arden. It had happened
again and again that we had found ourselves together in the recesses of the Forest, and enchanting
beyond all speech had been those days and nights
of mingled talk and dreams.

The Poet is one of the friends whose coming is
peculiarly welcome because it always harmonizes
with the mood of the moment, and no speech is
needed to bring us into agreement. Rosalind took
the visitor into our plan at once, and urged him to
go with us on this mysterious journey ; whereupon
he told us that, by one of those delightful coinci-
dences which are always happening to people of
kindred tastes and aims, this very errand had
brought him to our door. The time had come, he
said, when he could no longer resist the longing for
Arden ! We all smiled at that sudden outburst ;
how well we knew what it meant ! After months of
going our ways dutifully in the dust and heat of the
world, the longing for Arden would on the instant
become irresistible. Come what might, the hunger
for perfect comprehension and fellowship, the thirst
for the beauty and repose of the deep woods, must
be satisfied, and forsaking whatever was in hand we
fled incontinently across the invisible boundaries
into that other and diviner country. No sooner had
the Poet made his confession than we hastened to
make ours, and, without further consideration, we
resolved the very next day to shake the dust from

our feet and escape into Arden. This question
settled, a great gayety seized us, and we began to
plan new journeys for the years to come ; journeys
which had this peculiar charm—that they belonged
to a few kindred spirits ; the world knows nothing
of them, and when some obscure reference brings
them to mind, smiles its skeptical smile, and goes
on with its money-getting. Rosalind drew from its
hiding-place the chart of this world of the imagination which we were given to studying on long winter evenings, and of which only a few copies exist.
These charts are among the few things not to be
had for money ; if they fall into alien hands they
are incomprehensible. It is true of them, as of the
books which describe the Forest of Arden, that they
have a kind of second meaning, only to be discerned by those whose eyes detect the deeper things
of life. It is another peculiarity of these charts
that while science has indirectly done not a little
for their completeness, the work of preparing them
has fallen entirely into the hands of the poets ; not,
of course, the writers of verse alone, but those who
have had the vision of the great world as it lies in
the imagination, and who have heard that deep
and incommunicable music which sings at the heart
of it.

Rosalind spread this chart on the table, and we
drew our chairs around it, noting now one and now
another of the famous places of which all men
have heard, but which to most men are mere fig-

ments of dreams. Here, for instance, in a certain latitude plainly marked on the margin, is that calm sweet land of the Phæacians where reigns Alcinoüs the great-souled king, and the white-armed Nausicaä sings after her bath on the river's brink :

> Without the palace court and near the gate
> A spacious garden of four acres lay ;
> A hedge inclosed it round, and lofty trees
> Flourished in generous growth within—the pear
> And the pomegranate, and the apple tree
> With its fair fruitage, and the luscious fig,
> And olive always green.   The fruit they bear
> Falls not, nor ever fails in winter time
> Nor summer, but is yielded all the year.
> The ever-blowing west wind causes some
> To swell and some to ripen ; pear succeeds
> To pear ; to apple, apple, grape to grape,
> Fig ripens after fig.

Here, as Rosalind moves her finger, lies the valley of Avalon, whither Arthur went to heal his overmastering sorrow, and where the air is always sweet with the smell of apple blossoms. In this deep wood lives Merlin, still weaving, as of old, the magic spells.   There is the castle of the Grail, and as our eyes fall on it, suddenly there comes a hush, and we seem to hear the sublime antiphony, choir answering choir in heavenly melody, as Parsifal raises the cup, and the light from above smites it into sudden glory.   We are traveling eastward, touching here and there those names which belong only to the greatest poetry, when Rosa-

lind's finger—the index of our wanderings—suddenly pauses and rests on an island, not large, as it
lies amid that silent sea, but wonderful above all
islands to which thought has ever wandered or where
imagination has ever made its home. Under the light
of the lamp, with Rosalind's face bending over it,
no island ever slept in a deeper calm than this little
circle of land about which the greatest of the poets
once evoked the most marvelous of tempests.
Rosalind's finger does not move from that magical
point, and, peering on the chart, our eyes suddenly
meet, and a single thought is in them all. Why
not postpone Arden for the moment and explore
the isle of Miranda's morning beauty and Prospero's magical wisdom ?

" Why not ? " says Rosalind, speaking aloud, and
instead of answering her question the Poet and I
are wondering why we have never gone before.
Straightway we fall to studying the map more
closely ; we note the latitude and longitude ; it is
but a little way from the mainland where stretches
the green expanse of the Forest of Arden. We
might have gone long ago if we had been a little
more adventurous ; at least we think we might at
the first blush ; but when we talk it over, as we
proceed to do when Rosalind has rolled up the chart
and put it in its place, we are not quite so sure
about it. It is one of the singular things about this
kind of journeying that one learns how to travel
and where to go only by personal observation. Be-

fore we went to Arden, for instance, we had no
clear knowledge of any of these countries ; we had
often heard of them ; their names were often on
our lips ; but they were not real to us.   That happy
day when Arden ceased to be a dream to us was
the beginning of a rapid growth of knowledge concerning these invisible countries ; one by one they
seemed to rise within the circle of our expanding
experience until we became aware that we were
masters of a new kind of geography.   That delightful discovery was not many years behind us, but
this new knowledge had already become so much a
part of our lives that we often confused it with the
knowledge of commoner things.

That night, before we parted, our plans were completed ; on the morrow, when night came, the fire
on the hearth would be unlighted, for we should be
on Prospero's island.

II.

O, rejoice

Beyond a common joy ; and set it down
With gold on lasting pillars : in one voyage
Did Claribel her husband find at Tunis ;
And Ferdinand, her brother, found a wife
Where he himself was lost; Prospero, his dukedom,
In a poor isle; and all of us, ourselves,
Where no man was his own.

"HONEST Gonzalo never spoke truer word," said

the Poet, answering Rosalind who had been quot-
ing the old counselor's summing up of the common
good fortune on the island when Prospero dispelled
his enchantments and the shipwrecked company
found themselves saved as by miracle. It was our
first evening on the island ; one of those memorable
nights when all things seem born anew into some
larger heritage of beauty. The moon hung low
over the quiet sea, sleeping now under the spell of
the summer night, as if no storm had ever vexed it.
So silent, so hushed was it that but for the soft rip-
ple on the sand we should have thought it calmed
in eternal repose. Far off along the horizon the
stars hung motionless as the sea ; overhead they
shone out of the measureless depths of space with
a soft and solemn splendor. Not a branch moved
on the great trees behind us, folded now in the
universal mystery of the night. The little stretch
of beach, over whose yellow sands the song of the
invisible Ariel once floated, lay in the soft light fit
for the feet of fairies, or the gentle advance and retreat of the sea. The very air, suffused through all
that vast immensity with a mysterious light, seemed
like a dream of peace.

In such a place, at such an hour, one shrinks
from speech as from the word that breaks the spell.
When one is so much a part of the sublime order of
things that the universal movement of force that
streams through all things embraces and thrills him
with the consciousness of common fellowship, how

vain is all human utterance !   The greatest of
poems, the sublime harmony in which all things are
folded, has never been spoken, and never will be.
No lyre in any human hand will ever make those
divine chords audible.   The poets hear them, know
them, live by them ; but no verse contains them.
So much a part of that wondrous night were we that
any speech would have seemed like a severance of
things that were one ; all the deep meaning of the
hour was clear to us because we were included in it.
How long we sat in that silence I do not know ; we
had forgotten the world out of which we had
escaped, and the route by which we came ; we
knew only that an infinite sea of beauty and wonder
rippled on the beach at our feet, and that over us
the heavens were as a delicate veil, beyond which
diviner loveliness seemed waiting on the verge of
birth.

It was Rosalind who spoke at last, and spoke in
words which flashed the human truth of the hour
into our thoughts.   On this island we had found
ourselves ; so often lost, at times so long forgotten,
in the busy world that lay afar off.   And then we
fell a-talking of the island and of all the kindred
places where men have found homes for their souls ;
sweet and fragrant retreats whence the noise of
strife and toil died into a faint murmur, or was lost
in some vast silence.   At Milan, Prospero found the
cares of state so irksome, the joy of " secret
studies " so alluring, that, despairing of harmoniz-

ing things so alien, he took refuge with his books, and found his "library was dukedom large enough." But the problem was not solved by this surrender ; out of the library, as out of the dukedom, he was set adrift, homeless and friendless, until he set foot on the island where he was to rule with no divided sway. Here was his true home ; here the spirits of the air and the powers of the earth were his ministers ; here his word seemed part of the elemental order ; he spoke and it was done, for the winds and the sea obeyed him. And when, in the working out of destiny which he himself directed, he returns to the dukedom from which he had been thrust out, he is no longer the Prospero of ineffective days. Henceforth he will rule Milan as he rules the quiet dukedom of his books ; he has become a master of life and time, and his sovereignty will never again be disputed.

Prospero did not find the island ; he created it. It was the necessity of his life that he should fashion this bit of territory out of the great sea, that here his soul might learn its strength and win its freedom ; that here, far from dukedom and courtiers, he might discover that a great soul creates its own world and lives its own life. Milan may cast him out, as did Florence another of his kind, but this human rejection will but bring him into that empire which no enmity may touch, in the calm of whose divinely ordered government treasons are unknown. No man finds himself until he has created

a world for his own soul ; a world apart from care
and weakness and the confusions of strife, in which
the faiths that inspire him and the ideals that lead
him are the great and lasting verities.   To this
world-building all the great poetic minds are driven;
within this invisible empire alone can they reconcile the life that surrounds them with the life
that floats like a dream before them.   No great
mind is ever at rest until in some way the Real and
the Ideal are found to be one.   Literature is full of
these beautiful homes of the soul, reared without
the sound of chisel or hammer by the magic of the
Imagination—divinest of the faculties, since it is
the only one which creates.   The other faculties
observe, record, compare, combine ; the imagination alone uses the brush, the chisel, or the pen !

If one were to record these kingdoms of the
mind, how long and luminous would be the catalogue !   The golden age and the fabled Atlantis of
the elder poets; the "Republic" of the broad-
browed Athenian ; the secret gardens, impregnable
castles, sweet and inaccessible retreats of the medi-
æval fancy ; the Paradise of Dante ; the enchanting world through which the Fairy Queen moves ;
the "Utopia" of the noble More ; the Forest of
Arden—what visions of peace, what glimpses of
beauty, accompany every name ! To all these
worlds of supernal loveliness there is a single key ;
fortunate among men are they who hold it !

III.

Be not afraid ; the isle is full of noises,
Sounds and sweet airs that give delight and hurt not.
Sometimes a thousand twanging instruments
Will hum about mine ears ; and sometimes voices,
That, if I then had waked after long sleep,
Will make me sleep again ; and then, in dreaming,
The clouds methought would open, and show riches
Ready to drop upon me ; that, when I waked,
I cried to dream again.

WHEN the sun rose the next morning, we rose
with it, eager to explore our little world about which
the sea never ceased to sing its mighty hymn of
solitude and mystery. There was something impressive in the consciousness of our isolation ; between us and any noise of human occupation the
waters were stretched as a barrier against which all
sound died into silence. There was something
enchanting in the beauty and strangeness of this
tiny continent, unreported by any geography, un-
marked on any chart save that which a few possess
as a kind of sacred heritage, untraveled as yet by our
eager feet. There was something thrilling in the
associations that touched the island with such a light
as never fell from sun or star. With beating hearts
we set out on that wondrous exploration. Who
does not remember the thrill of the first discovery
of a new world ; that joy of the soul in possession
of a great new truth which passes all speech ?

There are hours in this troubled life when the mists are lifted and float away like faint clouds against the blue, and the great world lies like a splendid vision before us, and "the immeasurable heavens break open to the highest," and in a sudden rift of human limitation the whole sublime order opens before us, sings to us out of the fathomless depths of its harmony, thrills us with a sudden sense of God and of the undiscovered range and splendor of our lives ; and when they have passed, these hours remain with us in the afterglow of clearer vision and deeper faith. Such hours are the peculiar joy of those who hold the key of the imagination in their grasp and are able to unlock the gate of dreams, or make themselves the companion of the great explorers in the realms of truth and beauty. These are the secret joys which people solitude and make the quiet days one long draught of inspiration.

In such a mood our quest began and ended. We skirted the beach ; we plunged deep into the recesses of the woods ; we stretched ourselves on the broad expanse of greensward in the shade of the great boughs ; we followed the rivulet to the hushed and shadowy solitude where it issued from the moss-grown rock ; wherever we bent our steps the song of the sea followed us, and the day was calm and cool as with its breadth and freshness. The island had its own beauty ; the beauty of virgin forests and untrodden paths, of a certain fragrant sweetness gathered in years of untroubled solitude, of a certain pastoral repose such as comes to Nature when man is remote ; but that which gave us the thrill of something strangely sweet and satisfying, something apart from the world we had left, was not anything we saw with eye. All that was visible was beautiful, but it was a loveliness not unfamiliar ; it was the invisible continually breaking in upon our consciousness that laid us under a spell. We were conscious of something lovelier than we saw ; a world not to be discerned by sight, but real and unspeakably beautiful to the soul. Even to Caliban the isle was "full of noises "; "sounds and sweet airs that give delight" did not escape his brutish sense. Sometimes "a thousand twangling instruments " hummed about his ears ; sometimes voices whose soft music was akin to sleep floated about him ; and sometimes the clouds "would open and show riches ready to drop upon " him. There was a sweet enchantment in the air to which the dullest could not be indifferent. It hovered over us like some finer beauty, just beyond the vision of sense, and yet as real, almost as tangible, as the things we touched and saw.

Alone as we were upon the little island, we felt the diviner world of which that tiny bit of earth was part ; we knew the higher beauty of which all that visible loveliness was but a sign and symbol. The song of the sea, breathed from we knew not what depths of space, was not more real than this melody, haunting the island and dropping from the

air like blossoms from a ripening tree. Turn where
we would, this music went with us; it mingled with
the murmur of the trees; it blended with the limpid
note of the rivulet; it melted with the breeze that
swept across the grassy places. All day, and for
many another day, we were conscious of a larger
world of harmony and beauty folding in our little
world of tree and soil; we lived in it as freely and
made it ours as fully as the bit of earth beneath our
feet. Through all our talk this thread of melody
was run, and our very thoughts were set to this unfailing music. In those days the Poet wrote no
verses; what need of verse when poetry itself, that
deep and breathing beauty of the soul of things,
filled every hour and overflowed all the channels of
thought and sense !

But if we were dumb in the hearing of a music
beyond our mastery, we were not blind to the
parable conveyed in every sound and sight; in
those delicious days and nights a great truth
cleared itself forever in our minds. We know
henceforth how all dream-worlds, all beautiful
hopes and visions and ideals, are fashioned. They
are not of human making; they but make visible
things which already exist unseen; they but make
audible sounds which are already vocal unheard.
He who dreams, sleeps, and another fills the cham-
ber of his brain with moving figures; he who aspires,
hopes and believes, unlocks the door, and another
world, already furnished with beauty, lies before

him. Our ideals are God's realities. We build
the new worlds of our knowledge out of the dust of
worlds already swinging in space ; the stately
homes of our imagination rise on foundations of
the common earth. Prospero's island was made of
common soil; flowers, trees, and grass grow on it
as they grow about the homes of work and care.
The same sea washes its shores which beats upon
the coasts of ancient continents ; over it bends
that same sky which enfolds all the generations of
men. Prospero's island is no mirage, hovering
unreal and evanescent on the far horizon ; no impalpable phantom of reality floating like some
strayed flower on the lovely sea of dreams. It is
as solid as the earth, as real as the soul that fashioned it. No miracle was wrought, no law violated,
in its making. Beautiful, true, and enduring, it lies
upon the waters ; a haven for men in the storms
that beat upon the high seas of this troubled life.
That which is strange and wonderful about it is the
music which forever hovers about it ; that which
makes it enchanted ground is the sound of voices
sweet as the quietness of sleep, the vision of clouds
ready to drop unmeasured riches ! An island solid
as the great world out of which it was fashioned,
but sweet with heavenly voices and sublime with
heavenly visions—such is the island of Prospero's
enchantments.

And such are all true ideals, dreams, and aspirations. They have their roots in the same earth

whence the commonest weed grows ; but the light and life of the heavens are theirs also. In them the visible and the invisible are harmonized ; in them the real finds its completion in the ideal. The common earth is common only to those who are deaf to the voices and blind to the visions which wait on it and make its flight a music and its path a light. Out of these common things the great artists build the homes of our souls. Rock-founded are they, and broad-based on our mother earth : but they have windows skyward, and there, above the tumult of the little earth, the great worlds sing.

IV.

> You do yet taste
> Some subtilities o' the isle, that will not let you
> Believe things certain.

ONE brilliant morning, the sky cloudless and the sea singing under a freshening wind, we sat under a great tree, with a bit of soft sward before us, and talked of Prospero. In that place the master presence was always with us ; there was never an hour in which we did not feel the spell of his creative spirit. We were always secretly hoping that we should come upon him in some secluded place, his staff unbroken, and his book undrowned. But what need had we of sight while the island encompassed us and the multitudinous music filled the air ?

On that fair morning the magical beauty of the world possessed us, and our talk, blending unconsciously with the music of the invisible choir, was broken by long pauses. The Poet was saying that the world thought of Prospero as a magician, a wonder-worker, whose thought borrowed the fleetness of Ariel, whose staff unleashed the tempest and sent it back to its hiding-place when its work was done, and in whose book were written all manner of charms and incantations. This was the Prospero whom Caliban knew, and this is the Prospero whom the world remembers. " For myself," said he, " I often try to forget the miracles, so stained and defiled seem the great artists by this homage which is only another form of materialism. The search for signs and wonders is always vulgar ; it defiles every great spirit who compromises with it, because it puts the miracle in place of the truth. That which gives a wonder its only dignity and significance is the spiritual power which it evidences and the spiritual knowledge which it conveys. To the greatest of teachers this hunger for miracles was a bitter experience ; he who came with the mystery of the heavenly love in his soul must have felt defiled by the homage rendered as to a necromancer, a doer of strange things. The curiosity which draws men to the masters of the arts has no real honor in it ; the only recognition which is real and lasting is that which springs from the perception of truth and beauty disclosed anew in some noble

form.   Prospero was a magician, but he was much
more and much greater than a wonder-worker ; not
Caliban, but Ferdinand and Miranda and Gonzalo,
are the true judges of his power.   Prospero was the
master spirit of the world which moved about him.
He alone knew its secret and used its forces ; on
him alone rested the government of this marvelous
realm.   His command had stirred the seas and sent
the winds abroad which brought Milan and Naples
within his hand ; at his bidding the isle was full of
sounds ;   Ariel served him with tireless devotion ;
he read the sweet thought that flashed from Miranda to Ferdinand ;   he unearthed the base con-
spiracy of Caliban, Trinculo, and Stephano ;   he
read the treacherous hearts of Antonio and Sebas-
tian ;   in his hand all these threads were gathered,
and upon all these lives his will was imposed.   In
that majestic drama of human character and action,
powers of air and earth, the highest and the lowest
alike serving, it is a lofty soul and a noble mind
possessed by a great purpose, which control and tri-
umph.   The magical arts are simply the means by
which a great end is served ;   when the work is accomplished, the staff will be broken and the book
sunk beneath the sea, lower than any sounding of
plummet."

"Yes," said Rosalind impulsively, carrying the
thought another step forward, " Prospero deals with
natural, substantial things for great, real ends, not
with magical powers for fantastic purposes.   When

it falls in his way, he evokes forces so unusual that
they seem supernatural to those who do not
understand his power, but the end which lies before him is always real, enduring, and noble;
something which belongs to the eternal order of
things."

" For that matter," I interrupted, " it grows more
and more difficult to distinguish between the forces
and the achievements that we have thought real and
possible, and those which have seemed only dreams
and visions. Men are doing things every day by
mechanical agencies which the most famous of the
old magicians failed to accomplish. The visions of
great minds are realities discovered a little in advance of their universal recognition."

" As I was saying," continued the Poet, " most
men hold Prospero to be a mere wonder-worker, a
magician who puts his arts on and off with his
robe; they do not know that he stands for the
greatest force in the world. For the Imagination is
not only the inspiring leader of men in their strange
journey through life, but their nearest, most constant, and most practical helper and sustainer.
That our souls would have starved without the
Imagination we are all, I think, agreed; without
Imagination we should have seen and remembered
nothing on our long journey but the path at our
feet. The heavens above us, the great, mysterious
world about us, would have meant no more to us
than to the birds and the beasts that have perished

without thought or memory of the beauty which has encompassed them. All this the Imagination has interpreted for us. It has fashioned life for us, and the dullest mind that plods and counts and dies is ministered to and enriched by it. It does magical things. It puts on its robe and opens its book, and straightway the heavens rain melody and drop riches upon us. But this is its play. In these displays of its art it hints at the resources at its command, at the marvels it will yet bring to pass. Meanwhile it has made the earth hospitable for us and taught men how to live above the brutes."

The Poet stopped abruptly, as if he had been caught in the act of preaching, and Rosalind gave the sermon a delightful ending.

" I wonder," she said, " if love would be possible without the Imagination ? For the heart of love is the perception of a deep and genuine fellowship of the soul, and the end of love is the happiness which comes through ministry. Could we understand a human soul or serve it if the Imagination did not aid us with its wonderful light? Is it not the Imagination which enables me to put myself in another's place, and so to sympathize with another's sorrow and share another's joy ? Could a man feel the sufferings of a class or a race or the world if the Imagination did not open these things to him ? And if he did not understand, could he serve ?"

No one answered these questions, for they made

us aware on the instant how dependent are all the deep and beautiful relations of life on this wonderful faculty. But for this "master light of all our seeing," how small a circle of light would lie about our feet, how vast a darkness would engulf the world !

---

v.

> O wonder !
> How many goodly creatures are there here !
> How beauteous mankind is ! O brave new world,
> That has such people in't !

WE had never thought of the island in the old days save as lashed by tempests ; but now the suns rose and set, dawn wore its shining veil and night its crest of stars, and not a cloud darkened the sky; we seemed to be in the heart of a vast and changeless calm. There was no monotony in the unbroken succession of the days, but the changes were wrought by light, not by darkness. The singing of the sea, never rising into those shrill upper notes which bode disaster, nor sinking into the deep lower tones through which the awful thunder of the elements breaks, came to us as out of the depths of an infinite repose. The youth of an untroubled world was in it. The joy of effortless activities breathed through it. We felt that we were once more in the morning of the world's day, and hope gave the keynote to all our thought. Life is divided between hope and memory; when memory holds the chief place, the shadows are lengthening and the day declining.

It was one of the pleasures of the island that we were alone upon it. There was no trace of any other human occupation, although we never forgot those who had been before us in these enchanting scenes. One morning, when we had been talking about the delight of seclusion, Rosalind said that, although the silence and repose were really medicinal, people had never seemed so attractive to her as now when she remembered them under the spell of the island. It seemed to her, as she recalled them now, that the dull people had an interest of their own, the vulgar people were not without dignity, nor the bad people without noble qualities. The Poet, who had evidently been giving himself the luxury of dreaming, declared that we cannot know people save through the Imagination, and that lack of Imagination is at the bottom of all pessimism in philosophy, religion, and personal experience. A fact taken by itself and detached from the whole of which it is part is always hard, bare, repellant; it must be seen in its relations if one would perceive its finer and inner beauty; and it is the Imagination alone which sees things as a whole. The theologians who have stuck to what they call logic have spread a veil of sadness over the world which the poets must dissipate. " I do not mean," he added,

" that there are not somber and terrible aspects of life, but that these things have been separated from the whole, and discerned only in their bare and crushing isolated force. The real significance of things lies in their interpretation, and the Imagination is the only interpreter."

I had often had the same thought, and found infinite consolation in it; indeed, I rested in it so securely that I would trust myself with far more confidence to the poets than to the logicians. The guess of a great poetic mind has as solid ground under it as the speculation of a scientist; it differs from the scientific theory only in that it is an induction from a greater number of significant facts. The Imagination follows the arc until it "comes full circle"; observation halts and waits for further sight.

Rosalind thought it very beautiful that Miranda's first glance at men should have discovered them so fair and noble; there was evil enough in some of them, but standing beside Prospero Miranda saw only the "brave new world." I remembered at that moment that even Caliban discloses to the Imagination the germ of a human development; has not another poet written his later story and recorded the birth of his soul? It was characteristic of Rosalind that she should see the people in the marvelous drama through Miranda's eyes, and that straightway the whole world of men and women should reveal itself to her in a new light. " To see

the good in people," she said, " is not so much a
matter of charity as of justice. Our judgments of
others fail oftenest through lack of Imagination.
We fail to see all the facts ; we see one or two very
clearly, and at once form an opinion. To see the
whole range of a human character involves an intellectual and spiritual quality which few of us possess.
There is so little justice among us because we possess so little intelligence. I ought not to pronounce
judgment on a fellow-creature until I know all that
enters into his life ; until I can measure all the
forces of temptation and resistance ; until I can
give full weight to all the facts in the case. In
other words, I am never in a position to judge
another."

The Poet evidently assented to this statement,
and I could not gainsay it; is there not the very
highest authority for it ? The time will come when
there will be a universal surrender of that authority
which we have been usurping all these centuries.
We shall not cease to recognize the weakness and
folly of men, but we shall cease to decide the exact
measure of personal responsibility. That is a func-
tion for which we were never qualified ; it is a task
which belongs to infinite wisdom. The Imagination
helps us to understand others because it reveals the
vast compass of the influences that converge on every
human soul like the countless rivulets that give the
river its volume and impetus. To look at men and
women through the vision of the Imagination is to

see a very different race than that which meets our common sight. To this larger vision, within which the past supplements the present, the great army of men and women moves to a solemn and appealing music. The pathos of life touches them with an indescribable dignity ; the work of life gives them an unspeakable nobility. Under the meanest exterior there are one knows not what tragedies of denied hopes and unappeased longings ; behind the mask of evil there shines one knows not what struggling virtue overborne by impulses that flow from the past like irresistible torrents. Hidden under all manner of disguises—weakness, poverty, ignorance, vulgarity—there waits a world of ideals never realized but never lost ; the fire of aspiration burns in a thousand thousand souls that are maimed and broken, bruised and baffled, but which still survive. Is not this the unquenchable spark that some day, in freer air, shall break into white flame ? It is the Imagination only that discerns in a thousand contradictions, a thousand obscurities, the large design to be revealed when the ring of the hammer has ceased, the dust of toil been laid, the scaffolding removed, and the finished structure suddenly discloses the miracle wrought among those who were blind.

VI.

I might call him
A thing divine ; for nothing natural
I ever saw so noble.

ROSALIND was deeply interested in Prospero ; and when the Poet and I had talked long and eagerly about him, she often threw into the current some comment or suggestion that gave us quite another and clearer view of his genius and work. But at heart Rosalind's chief interest was in Miranda and Ferdinand. The presence of Prospero had given the island a solemn and far-reaching significance in the geography of the world ; Miranda and Ferdinand had left an unfailing and beguiling charm about the place. If we could have known the point where these two fresh and unspoiled natures met, I am confident we should have stayed there by common but unspoken consent. After all our discoveries in this mysterious world, youth and love remain the first and sweetest in our thoughts : there is nothing which takes their place, nothing which imparts their glow, nothing which conveys such deep and beautiful hints of the better things to be. Miranda had known no companionship but her father's, no world but the sea-encircled island, no life but the secluded and eventless existence in that wave-swept solitude. She had had the rare good fortune to ripen under the spell of pure, high thoughts, and so near to

Nature that no grosser currents of influence h‍
borne her away from the most wholesome and co‍.
soling of all companionships. Ferdinand came
from the shows of royalty and small falsities of
courtiers ; the palace, the city, the crowded, self-
seeking, hypocritical world had encompassed him
from youth, robbed him of privacy, cheated him of
that repose which brings a man to a knowledge of
himself, and despoils him of those sweet and tranquilizing memories which grow out of a quiet childhood as the wild flowers spring along the edges of
the woods.

Coming, one from the stillness of a solitary island
and the other from the roar and rush of a court and
a city, these two met, and there flashed from one to
the other that sudden and thrilling intelligence
which on the instant gives life a new interpretation and the world an all-conquering loveliness.
Nowhere, surely, has the eternal romance found
more significant setting than on this magical island,
about which sea and sky, day and night, weave and
weave again those vanishing webs of splendor in
which daybreak and evening stars are snared ; with
such music throbbing on the air as invisible spirits
make when the command of the master is on
them ! Here, surely, was the home of this drama
of the soul, the acting of which on the troubled
stage of life is a perpetual appeal to faith and hope
and joy ! For youth and love are shining words in
the vocabulary of the Imagination—words which

contain the deepest of present and predict the
sweetest of future happiness. So deeply interwoven is the real significance of these words with
the Imagination that, separated from it, they lose
all their magical glow and beauty. Youth moves
in no narrow territory ; its boundary lines fade out
into infinity. It feels no iron hand of limitation ;
it discerns no impassable wall of restriction. Life
stretches away before and about it limitless as space
and full of unseen splendors as the stars that crowd
and brighten it. The great wings of hope, un-
bruised yet by any beatings of the later tempests,
shine through the air, lustrous and tireless, as if all
flights were possible. And far off, on the remote
horizon lines where sight fails, the mirage of dreams
dissolves and reappears in a thousand alluring
forms.

Love knows even less of limitation and infirmity.
Its eyes, sometimes oblivious of the things most obvious, pierce the remotest future, read the innermost soul, discern the last and highest fruitions.
The seed in its hand, hard, black, unbroken, is
already a flower to its thought; out of the bare,
stern facts of the present its magical touch brings
one knows not what of joy and loveliness. And
when youth and love are one, the heavens are not
bright enough for their thoughts, nor eternity long
enough for their deeds. Amid the shadows of life
they seem to have caught a momentary radiance
from beyond the clouds ; amid sorrows and sins and

all manner of weariness they are the recurring vision and revelation of the eternal order. All the world waits on them and rejoices in them ; and the bitter knowledge of what lies before the eager feet, waiting with passionate hope on the threshold, does not lessen the perennial interest in that fair picture; for in youth and love are realized the universal ideals of men. Youth and love are the mortal synonyms of immortality ; all that freshness of spirit, buoyancy of strength, energy of hope, boundlessness of joy, completeness and glory of life, imply, are typified in these two things, always vanishing and yet always reappearing among men. Wearing the beautiful masks of youth and love, the gods continually revisit the earth, and in their luminous presence faith forever rebuilds its shattered temples.

That which makes youth and love so precious to us is the play they give to the Imagination ; indeed, the better part of them both is compounded of Imagination. The horizons recede from their gaze because the second sight of Imagination is theirs— that prescience which pierces the mists which enfold us, and discerns the vaster world through which we move for the most part with halting feet and blinded eyes. Youth knows that it was born to life and power and exhaustless resources ; love knows that it has found and shall forever possess those beautiful ideals which are the passion of noble natures.

Are they blind, these flower-crowned, joy-seeking figures ; or are we blind who smile through tears at their illusions? On this island there is but one answer to that question ; for do we not know that they only who believe and trust discern the truth, and that to faith and hope alone is true vision given? "As yet lingers the twelfth hour and the darkness, but the time will come when it shall be light, and man will awaken from his lofty dreams and find—his dreams all there, and that nothing is gone save his sleep."

THE END.